# PRAISE FOR THE NOVELS OF ANDY STRAKA

# SPLIT
# CITY

# SPLIT CITY

Andy Straka

Clovercroft Publishing

Split City: A Jesus Spares Mystery

© 2021 by Andy Straka

Published by Clovercroft Publishing, Franklin, Tennessee

Published in association with Larry Carpenter of
Christian Book Services, LLC
www.christianbookservices.com

Edited by Christy Callahan

Cover and Interior Layout Design by Suzanne Lawing

Printed in the United States of America

978-1-954437-17-3

# 1

In bowling, as the old joke goes, there is never a good time to clean the gutters. Likewise, I suppose, there is never a good time to visit the morgue.

Sheriff Reginald Lawton frowned at me in the antiseptic light.

"Why are you a cop?" I asked.

"What kind of a question is that?"

I'd always liked the man but wasn't too fond of his laser-like appraisal of me as we shook hands in the cold of the early morning. His coffee-colored eyes hinted of suspicion. His forehead tapered into huge brown ears. One of the ears had been partly lopped off, which had spawned all sorts of rumors about his past, because he'd been a police officer in the city years before.

"I don't know," I said. "I imagine this must be a stressful part of your work. That's all."

"Stress comes with the job." He grunted.

I didn't respond.

My name's Billy Gills. I'm a former pro bowler and co-owner of Split City Lanes, a classic hometown bowling alley in Twin Strikes, a charmingly rundown town in Partridgeberry County, a forgotten corner of the Catskill Mountains of Upstate New York. Which makes me about as far from being a cop as I am from picking up a 7-10 split.

The sheriff released my hand from his meaty grip. "Seems you're a little jumpy."

"Sorry," I said. "Never been through anything like this before."

"Of course." He raised an eyebrow. "But you also said you were certain this isn't who I think it is."

I nodded.

"How do you know that again?" he asked.

"Instinct." I tapped my head. "You know. Gut feeling."

"Right," he said, his tone dripping with sarcasm.

He clearly wasn't buying my schtick. But I needed to cling to something to push away my anxiety. We were standing, after all, in the entryway to the basement morgue tucked discreetly below the county medical examiner's office in our county seat of Partridgeberry where a rusted vent fan wheezed above the door.

The sheriff and I knew each through the occasional pickup basketball game at the public high school gym in Partridgeberry. I wasn't much of a hoop player my-self, and neither was he. But the sheriff was an unselfish and relentless competitor, a ferocious rebounder who set treelike screens and never hesitated to dive on the floor for a loose ball. We might have come from different geographic and racial backgrounds, but we shared the same competitive spirit and had grown to respect one another as casual acquaintances.

He used a key to open the lock on the morgue door. Leaving an otherwise pleasant May morning behind, I followed him into a short corridor lined with gunmetal gray lockers. The temperature in the hallway reminded me of the inside of my refrigerator. Which, I remembered, was badly in need of cleaning.

"I appreciate you coming down here so early, Billy," said the sheriff. "We don't usually have to go through this step for suicides. But, like I told you on the phone, considering your brother's so well known in the community, not to mention a major employer, I want to be careful about any public statement."

"I understand," I said. "But, like I told you on the phone, I don't think you need to worry about this being my brother."

I suppose I should mention at this point that I co-own Split City with my identical twin brother, Bo. Although Bo is our major investor, he's hardly ever there. A former pro bowler himself, he's made a fortune manufacturing funkily styled bowling shoes—TreadBos they're called—and related footwear. The factory is here in the county seat of Partridgeberry, about a half hour's drive from Twin Strikes.

The sheriff led me down the row and showed me where to hang my coat. He also showed me the personal protective gear I would need to go farther into the morgue—a mask, latex gloves, and a thin paper jumpsuit to go over my clothes. Which snapped me back to the reality that I was about to see a dead body.

Could this actually be Bo, despite my certainty that it wasn't? How would I feel if it were? For someone who'd spent his life hanging around bowling alleys, the mixed odor of a decomposing body and ammonia wasn't the worst thing I'd ever smelled, but it was bad enough. Maybe people who worked here got used to it. Same as I'd grown accustomed to the charming fragrances of bowling shoe disinfectant, petrified pizza, and backed up restroom toilets.

I struggled into the paper suit, looking for some tangible object to focus on.

"Are you okay?" the sheriff asked.

I nodded, although I was pretty sure he could tell my confidence was wavering.

"How many times have you tried calling your brother now since I contacted you?"

"I don't know," I said. "Three, four? Plus, I've sent him texts. But, like I said, he doesn't usually answer me right away. That's just Bo."

"When was the last time you saw him?" he asked.

"A week ago. He drove up to Twin Strikes to check on his boat and we met for lunch."

What I didn't tell the sheriff was that Bo and I had argued and that it hadn't ended well.

"And you haven't seen or talked to him since?"

"No. But, that's not unusual. Bo's not all that communicative sometimes. I swung by his condo on the way here. He wasn't home. Drove past the factory too, but the parking lot was empty."

"And yet you still want to stick with your intuition," he said.

"For now," I said, pushing back against the sudden tremor in my voice. "You said yourself the body was found outdoors without ID."

"True enough," he said.

"So, what makes you so sure this is Bo?"

"What do you think?" He shot me an incredulous glance. "Because I'm looking at you, Billy. You'll see."

I followed him through another door into a large, brightly lit space that looked like an end-of-the-world operating room. Moveable lamps hung like suspended satellites from the ceiling. Two prominent signs on the wall warned of the dangers of contacting contaminated body fluids. Three sides of the room were lined with stainless-steel shelves and clear glass doors, through which I could see an assortment of barbaric looking tools and instruments.

I took a deep breath. My mask was making it hard to breath. It reminded me of the time our mother forced Bo and me to wear matching clip-on bow ties when we were first graders. Mine'd felt like a chain hung around my neck. But Mom had practically squealed with delight at the sight of us in our identical outfits. She snapped photo after photo of Bo and me before hustling us off with our matching Batman lunch boxes to catch the bus to school.

"Is this it?" I asked.

"Yes," the sheriff said. "They'll be bringing the body in any second."

"Don't you just pull out a body drawer or something?"

"Nah. We're not exactly what I'd call a high-volume operation around here."

I supposed that was a good thing, although it didn't feel like it at the moment. The sheriff must have sensed my nervousness.

"Now is the worst part," he said. "Don't worry. This will soon be over…Here we go."

His voice seemed near yet far away. The way the theme park attendant sounds before pushing the button to send you off on the Twisting Twizzle of Peril thrill ride.

As if on cue, a bump sounded from across the room. A door on the opposite wall opened, and a technician, whose face was also hidden beneath a mask, wedged it open and backed into the room. He was helping to guide a gurney through the door. It was covered by a white sheet, just like you see in the movies. Another masked technician pushed from the other end.

With no preamble or ceremony, they rolled the body into the middle of the room. The sheriff nodded to one of the techs. The man leaned over the gurney, drew back the sheet, and we all stood there looking at the body.

I felt sick to my stomach. Though my twin and I hadn't exactly been best friends of late, there was no denying it now. At first glance, there could be little doubt whose dead body lay before us.

"I'm sorry you had to see this, Billy," the sheriff said.

I nodded dumbly. Had I been overconfident, too sure he was wrong?

The two techs stood mutely by. For them, I imagined there was some sort of morbid fascination in seeing me standing there, alive, hovering over my identical twin brother's remains. Like staring at life and death simultaneously through a mirror. This would be how I would look one day too, wasn't it? On somebody else's gurney.

"Seen enough?" the sheriff asked.

"Not yet," I told him.

I tried to come to terms with Bo being gone. In death, he looked like he might have been sleeping— except for the bloody gunshot wound below his right ear. There was no mistaking the Caucasian skin, high cheekbones, and slightly unusual shape of his nose, features I'd subconsciously catalogued over the years as also being my own.

But something wasn't right. His body also looked different, and his overall appearance triggered a memory, a faint impression that had nothing to do with Bo—of what, or whom, I couldn't recall.

"Something seems off here," I said.

The sheriff tried to slough it off. "Not a big surprise in these kinds of circumstances. We're waiting on toxicology results. See if he had any alcohol or drugs in his system."

I said nothing as I looked back over the gunshot wound to the head.

The eyes of the two technicians widened a little, waiting for my further reaction from behind their masks.

Then, as I paid even closer attention to the body, I began to notice more details that didn't seem to fit. The hair was different than Bo normally wore his. It also looked as if he'd suddenly put on a fair amount weight. Which, given Bo's fitness fanaticism and the fact I'd seen him only a week before, hardly seemed possible. I also noted some odd, burn-like marks on the fingers.

In a burst of inspiration, it dawned on me that I'd been right all along. This wasn't, in fact, my twin brother lying here on this gurney. Bo wasn't dead.

I broke into a grin beneath my mask, a reaction that took me by surprise. I was so relieved, I could have kissed the sheriff's head above his high and tight, very dope haircut.

The sheriff must have thought I'd lost my senses. "What's wrong with you?" he asked.

I probably looked like an idiot as I stood there beaming. But I downshifted quickly because it also dawned on me that this dead man, whoever he was, had almost fooled even me.

I sighed. "So, I see this man shot himself."

"Yes. Seems pretty straightforward on first examination. You can't miss the wound, of course. The ME will confirm cause of death. The gun was found in his hand. No fingerprints on it but his own."

I nodded.

"Well?" The sheriff's eyes seemed to form an urgent question mark above his mask.

"Well, what?"

"Can you confirm this is your brother, Bo Gills?" he asked. I suppose it was the official question he had to ask.

"No, sir," I said.

"What?" His eyes lifted in alarm.

"Sorry, Sheriff. Like I told you from the beginning, this isn't Bo."

# 2

The sheriff winced. He turned to his two morgue techs.

"Give us a minute here, will you, guys?"

The two men nodded and shrugged before departing the room.

I can't help but wonder if this was the moment where I first became an amateur detective. Maybe it was something that'd been lurking inside of me all along.

I'd been so intent on looking over the body, I suddenly realized I no longer felt sick. The sheriff, however, seemed less than enthusiastic about my newfound interest in his corpse.

"Okay, Billy. Give me a break. This man looks just like you and your brother. Unless you've got some long-lost triplet somewhere, he *must* be Bo."

I shook my head. "I'm telling you, Sheriff, it isn't my brother. He's a lookalike. A doppelgänger. I have no idea who he is."

"What makes you so sure?" At least he was willing to listen.

I pointed to the body. "First off, this guy's hair is longer and completely different than how Bo usually keeps his."

"Okay, so maybe your brother went and bought himself a hairpiece or something."

"I can't see Bo ever doing that."

"All right," he said, folding his arms across his chest. "So there may be the minor mystery of the hair."

"There's more," I said. "Bo keeps himself in top shape. He's pretty religious about it. Goes to the gym and works out nearly every day. Your man here looks like he's a good twenty pounds heavier than my brother. This guy, whoever he is, has been eating a lot of rich food."

Which, I had to admit, actually made him look a little more like me. I was carrying a little too much weight, especially by skinny jean standards.

The sheriff still seemed skeptical, but I could tell he was warming to the idea that maybe there was more to this situation than met the eye. Since the sheriff had served with the NYPD before retiring to Partridgeberry and running for sheriff, I imagined he'd seen his fair share of dead bodies. Outside of the occasional accidents and people dying of disease or old age, Partridgeberry County didn't see many fatalities. Most of the deceased went to Gattlin's funeral home a few blocks down the street.

"Can I ask you something else?"

"Of course," he said. "If it'll help you further iden-tify this body."

"How was this man dressed when he was found?"

The sheriff shrugged. "Pretty normal stuff of the kind you might buy at Walmart. Heavy pants, flan-nel shirt, work boots, and a cheap down jacket—all soaked in blood. We've got them bagged as evidence."

"No TreadBo shoes?"

He stared at me for a moment. Then he shook his head.

"That doesn't sound like Bo either. He always wears expensive clothes. And he wouldn't be caught dead—sorry about the pun—without his TreadBos."

"Yeah," the sheriff said. "A couple of times I've seen him dressed in some hyper cool outfits too. Like a Hollywood celebrity."

"That's Bo for you." I paused. "What about fingerprints?"

"Wait a minute," he said with an icy stare. "Who's questioning who here?"

"Sorry, Sheriff. Just trying to be of help."

"All right. Just so you know, we ran a quick check on the prints. Didn't find any on record. I assume your brother's never been arrested before?"

I shook my head. "Not to my knowledge."

"That would explain why no prints on record," he said. "But the fingertips look funny, like they've been scarred. Did your brother burn his hands recently?"

"Not that I know of. I don't normally pay attention to his fingertips when I see him."

"Sure. Anyway, we didn't want to have to wait for dental records or DNA, which is why I brought you down here."

"Did you know that identical twins share the same DNA but not the same fingerprints?" I asked him.

"No." A crease formed on his forehead. "I didn't know that. But if this isn't your brother, then you need to explain something else to me." He reached inside a folded notebook and pulled out a clear bag containing a plastic card with a prominent logo on it. "This was found on our dead man's body."

I recognized the TreadBo logo and knew right away what it was.

"You recognize it?"

"Of course," I said. "It's an office entry card from Bo's company, TreadBo."

"Yeah. And your brother's factory here in Partridgeberry just so happens to be right down the street from where this body was found."

"Where exactly was the body found?"

"In a secluded parking spot next to the river. Behind the old abandoned paper warehouse. One of our deputies making their rounds called it in."

I knew the place. Bo had once considered renting the warehouse back when his company was really booming. I tried to picture it.

"Did you check and see who the card is registered to?" I asked.

"Not yet. We're waiting until the factory opens for the first shift."

"Truly bizarre," I said, trying to think. This wasn't Bo. But who was he? And how did he get ahold of an office key card?

"You know I have it on pretty good authority that that debacle of a conference your brother sponsored up in Twin Strikes last month cost him and his company a boatload of money. Don't imagine it helped you or your bowling alley either."

I said nothing. He was right.

"Times are hard," he said. "And the word around town is the factory isn't doing all that well this year. Sudden financial pressure can turn anyone desperate. Your brother say anything to you about that when you saw him?"

"Yeah," I admitted. "I know he's lost a lot of money recently."

"You still want to stick with your story, then? You still want to try to tell me this isn't your brother lying here?"

The card was pretty strange. I had to give him that. And the money part was true. I looked over the body once again, cataloging every little feature, everything I knew about my brother's face.

"I'm telling you," I said again. "That's not Bo."

#

Out in the hall, we stripped off our jumpsuits and masks.

"I've been reading up on you guys since the body was called in," the sheriff said. "You and your brother used to be quite the touring pros."

He handed me his smartphone with the screen turned so I could read a digital copy of an article from an old issue of *Sporting News Today*. I guess he'd been thinking of what he was going to have to write for the sheriff's department press release.

"TWIN TERRORS OF TICONDEROGA" the story was titled. "BOWLING KINGPINS BILLY AND BO GILLS HAIL FROM UPSTATE NEW YORK."

Bo and I were in our bowling prime back then. Ranked eighth and ninth on the pro tour. We flip-flopped nearly every tournament, separated in the standings by mere hundredths of a point. But by the time Bo and I made the tour, pro bowling had come down quite a few notches from its heyday. Tournament purses weren't as large. Sponsorships were getting harder to come by since TV and other advertising revenue had begun to shrink. At least the identical twin angle gave the sportswriter something interesting to still scribble about in his article.

"I'm guessing you carved that story out of a fossilized tree bark somewhere," I said.

"Yeah, right. The two of you must've been making some pretty good money back then."

"Not as much as you might think."

Bo and I weren't from Ticonderoga, New York, either, although it might have been our closest big town. We grew up in a little speck of a place called Harlow. Nice enough people, but you wouldn't even know it was there if you missed the flashing yellow light or blinked when you drove through. The sportswriter thought Ticonderoga sounded better. Which was close enough, I suppose.

"Twenty-five years of police work, and I've never had identical twins where one of them was involved in a suicide before. You believe that?" he said absently.

I shrugged.

"Being on the road as much as you guys used to be must have been hard."

"Hard enough," I said.

"You or your brother ever do drugs?"

"No."

"How about heavy drinking?"

"Not me. I generally stick to beer and wine. And the occasional cigar."

"Maybe your brother was into something you didn't know about," he suggested. "Wouldn't be the first time someone was keeping secrets from family, believe me." His tone remained casual. Like he was just making conversation.

Was he beginning to suspect me or Bo of something? For the first time, I began to get a glimpse of the detective side of him. Quietly curious. Persistent and persuasive.

"I don't know what else to tell you," I said.

"Okay, try looking at the situation from my side," he said. "A guy looking like your brother shows up dead just down the street from his office carrying a key card from his own company. What would you think?"

"I guess I'd be thinking exactly what you seem to be thinking. But from my side of the table, I just saved you and your department from making a colossal, publicly embarrassing mistake."

"Maybe the emotion of the moment here is compromising your ability to confirm your twin's identity."

"No," I said. "No way."

"Uh-huh." He rubbed his chin. "Okay, Billy," he said." We'll play it your way for now."

# 3

## THE WEEKEND BEFORE

Bo had driven up from Partridgeberry to meet me for lunch in Twin Strikes. We met at the restaurant next door to the marina on the shore of our beautiful Lake Conostowakaka, where Bo's big cabin cruiser was out of dry dock and being prepared for the upcoming season.

"You look tired," I told him as we sat down across from one another.

"Observant as ever, Billy," he said sarcastically.

Despite his eccentricities and the fact that we often butted heads, I was secretly proud of my brother. The pro bowling circuit had long ago faded from the ranks of top paying professional sports. Bo and I both had made some decent money, but neither of us had raked in a huge fortune. As his pro career began to wind down, Bo had taken it upon himself to rethink something we both knew well: bowling shoes.

Taking his cue from basketball shoes, he designed the world's first line of high-top bowling footwear. Which, it was no coincidence, also happened to bear a certain resemblance to one of the widely popular basketball sneakers. For a few glorious years TreadBo bowling shoes became the Air Jordans of bowling. TreadBos ("shoes that roll") had come to dominate an eccentric but loyal corner of the bowling and shoe fashion world.

In case you're wondering, Twin Strikes, the name of the town where I lived and Split City was located, had nothing to do with Bo and me. According to local legend, the town had gotten its name from a pair of lightning bolts that had struck simultaneously on either side of the lake a couple of hundred years before. But the name Twin Strikes did make it seem like poetic destiny when my great uncle Shirley (yes, his name was Shirley) died and left ownership of Split City to Bo and me. Even if the enterprise was barely making a profit and didn't own its own building.

Bo was too busy with his growing shoe business to get involved. So, it had fallen to me to either shutter the business or move to Twin Strikes and figure out how to keep the alley afloat.

"What gives?" I asked.

"What do you think? We're still trying to bail ourselves out from the conference disaster. Sales are down. Money is tight. It's been horrible for the

TreadBo brand. I almost called you to cancel, but I wanted to come check on the boat." From our small window table, he looked out across the lake to the mountain beyond.

Unlike Twin Strikes, there was no local legend about how Lake Conostowakaka got its name. Although I did have to bounce a drunk out of Split City once who kept rambling on and on about it being a lost Iroquois word. I think the man was hallucinating. On the other hand, it might well have been that one of the guy's ancestors had gotten together for a beach party many centuries before with a couple of his native American pals. Who knows? They may have decided it was up to them to christen the lake. And, after a few gourds of rum, Conostowakaka could have sounded like the perfect name.

"Maybe you should try to slow down a little. Take some time off," I proposed.

"It's an idea," he said. "I could do another ironing trip."

I couldn't help but wonder sometimes if all of the money Bo'd made has gone to his head. Not long after he stopped bowling, for example, he took up a different kind of sport: extreme ironing.

In case you've never heard of extreme ironing, the goal of the game is to cart around an ironing board, engage in some sort of adventure activity such as mountain climbing, scuba diving, or bronco busting, and attempt to iron a piece of clothing while in the middle of whatever it is you are doing. Or, at the very least pose, for a mid-ironing photo in the most extreme or outlandish place possible, such as the top of a mountain or hanging from the side of a galloping horse. It may sound crazy, but people have pulled off all sorts of feats. Common ones included ironing while unicycling or skateboarding. Ironing while running a marathon was also a perennial favorite. Ditto for ironing on water skis.

Bo almost got himself killed once trying to pull off the feat while surfing when a wave flipped him over and the iron hit him in the head.

This may sound strange, but whenever I was around my brother, I felt like I was in two different worlds. I couldn't help but notice every little flaw in my twin's appearance—the angular shape of his ears, the unusually large hands and long fingers so like my own. The best way most people who didn't know us well could tell the two of us apart was by the way we dressed. He was insecure about the way he looked and was always trying out different combinations of clothing, often expensive, sometimes outlandish. Today he was decked out in bell bottom, hippy-tattered jeans and a muslin shirt from India, complete with beads around his neck. Not the kind of outfit you saw someone wearing every day in the Catskills.

"How is everything else going at the factory?" I asked.

"Great, Billy. Just great."

Things were always supposed to be doing great at TreadBo. Callers were greeted with, "It's a great day at TreadBo Shoes!" I usually liked the positivity, but sometimes it got on my nerves.

"Look at you," I said. "You sound like a walking Mr. Corporate."

He smirked. "Yeah. Right."

Despite the warming weather, there was still a chill in the air today. The restaurant was cool as well, and Bo seemed to be shivering a little. It reminded me of the year before when he'd ironed his entire day's laundry standing on a shrinking Lake Conostowakaka ice sheet.

"You don't seem yourself," I said. "Maybe you're depressed."

"I don't know what you're talking about."

"Sounds like denial to me," I chided.

"Stop it." He held up his hand. "I'm not depressed. I'm…I don't know what I am. I…"

"Maybe your celebrity star has been fading a little these past couple of years."

He sat back and folded his arms across his chest. Bo had indeed become something of a minor celebrity due to TreadBo. Now, maybe not so much.

Although I was sometimes jealous of Bo's wealth, I envied not his problems. The TreadBo factory was one of Partridgeberry county's largest employers. At one time the company had even made some list of America's fastest growing companies, and Bo had been featured in a national business magazine. Which shows why Sheriff Lawton had been so cautious about putting out any public information when he'd called me that morning. The TreadBo name may have grown a little long in the tooth of late, but there was still a funky cool weirdness to TreadBos some consumers and bowlers seemed to like.

Sometimes I wondered how my twin and I were ever able to get along. I was born four minutes before Bo. I imagined I must've shoved him out of the way in the womb and burst forth to say, *Hello, world!'* This singular moment in time must have impacted Bo in some indiscernible, visceral way that went beyond reason. Ever since then, he was having no more of coming in second.

"You know, except for the conference, we haven't seen much of you lately over at Split City," I said. "You should come over some night. We'll close down early and bowl. Just you and me on alternating lanes. Mano a mano. Like the old days."

"No way." Bo grunted in mock disgust. "I'm done with all of that."

"Really? Don't you ever miss it?" I asked.

"Miss what?"

"The competition."

He looked out the window and said nothing.

Our parents may have done everything in their power to make sure we were treated the same, but things were never equal as far as Bo and I were concerned. Arguing was our lifelong avocation. When we were growing up, our parents took us bowling every weekend, and we fought like demons to outdo one another when we competed. If I scored lower than Bo, I bit my lip and sulked. If Bo lost to me, he would usually end up kicking and screaming on the floor.

But even as adults, we could never truly get away from one another. We were like boxers hugging in a clinch who'd been thrown together in the ring of life, forever held in a magnetic dance.

"Are you ever really done, Bo?" I asked. "Last I looked, you and your company still made bowling shoes."

"Yeah. Right. We bowl together again, and some enterprising kid will probably take it as another opportunity to sneak in the back and shoot a video with his smartphone. Put it up on YouTube or something."

"All the better," I said. "It might help us recover from what happened last month so the factory can sell more TreadBos."

"Maybe," he said. "I don't know. I'm still trying to figure out what happened. I don't know if there's anything either of us can do right now to recover from that."

"Ah. Maybe it won't turn out so bad in the end."

He surprised me by slamming his hand on the table and glaring at me. "It's bad, Billy. It's really bad."

"Okay." I didn't know what else to say.

"Let's just shut up and eat our lunch."

The waitress came and took our orders for sandwiches.

# 4

ONE MONTH BEFORE

I had a hard time finding a parking spot in front of Split City that Sunday morning. Outside the alley entrance, people were already lining up at a hastily erected security checkpoint. Along the shoulder of the highway, a couple of media vehicles stood watch beneath a bright blue sky.

It was the final day of "The Split Down the Middle Weekend of Hope Colloquium." The brainchild of Bo and his TreadBo marketing director Addison Foley, the idea behind the conference was to bring together elected state officials of all political persuasions and their families for a preseason weekend of fun, bowling, and recreation around the lake. No politics. Just relaxation and fun.

Bo hoped the event would "encourage unity and cooperation in the crafting of public policy." He also saw it as a way of bringing some much-needed publicity to TreadBo and Split City, not to mention promoting tourism in Twin Strikes and Partridgeberry County.

And so far, it seemed to be working.

There'd been a farmer's market the afternoon before that included a face painter, potters, and other craft sellers, a couple of food trucks that'd driven down from Albany, and even baby goats for the kids. Saturday evening had featured a dinner with a diverse selection of ethnic foods and dancing at the resort. (TreadBo brought in a hip new reggae group to provide live music.)

Bo had also made a wise choice timing the conference during one of the first weekends of spring. While the region buzzed with tourists during the summer and fall leaf season, the rest of the year we locals pretty much had the place to ourselves. Which meant the politicians and their families had an unobstructed chance to enjoy the lake, the resort, and the town. It was still too cold for swimming, but fishing season had just opened.

Reportedly, a few of the politicians and/or their children had hauled in some large trout and smallmouth bass. Everyone seemed to agree that the Split Down the Middle Conference had been a big success. Which was a good thing, because as far as Split City was concerned, we needed all of the publicity we could get.

#

The bowling alley stood back from the road on a couple of scrubby acres at the edge of town. Despite some modest upgrades, investment in outward appearance, and better food, the place hadn't changed all that much since the day I bought the 1970s-era facility. To our regulars and a percentage of tourists, the old alley feel was part of Split City's allure. Some days when business was slow, however, I just hoped we weren't too much of an eyesore.

I climbed out of my beat-up Toyota 4Runner and smiled at the size of the crowd.

I looked up in time to spot my general manager, Petula Jenkins, desperately attempting to check people in through the front door.

"Billy," she called out. "There you are. We need all hands on deck here."

Her teeth may not have been fully straight, but her full cheeks and ample chin rose into an adorable dimple when she smiled. Which revealed how big her heart was. Over the years she'd worked for me, Petula had become, in many ways, the big sister I wished I'd always had.

"Good morning," I said. "I thought you said the service wasn't supposed to start until eleven."

"I know. I know. But today is different."

Once a month, Split City also hosted Jesus Spares, a non-denominational church service followed by three hours of free food and free bowling. Petula was a volunteer assistant pastor at our local nondenominational church. She and the lead pastor, Reverend Al, had conceived of the idea of Jesus Spares as an outreach and gathering of souls from all over the region who would come one Sunday a month for an event that included food and bowling paid for by her congregation. The church, along with a couple of social service organizations, even sponsored a busload of people who rode up from the city.

Since the two events happened to be scheduled for the same weekend, Bo thought it was a good idea to incorporate Jesus Spares into his Split Down the Middle Weekend for any who wished to attend. Following the church service, he planned for the conference to come to a peaceful and fun climax with a "Bowling for Unity" social and food event at Split City. Reverend Al and Petula had been reluctant, at first, to allow Jesus Spares to be associated with the conference, especially since a number of elected officials would be in attendance. But they'd eventually gone along with Bo's wishes, on the condition that, like the rest of the weekend, no politicking would be allowed.

The charter bus from the city appeared, and a couple of volunteers from the church rushed over to greet the people and help the driver find a place to park. Which unfortunately left Petula alone to try to deal with the crowd.

"Are you all right?" I asked her as came around the back of the check-in desk.

"Yes. Just busy. There are more people here than we expected."

"Where's Reverend Al?"

"One of the teens from the church had to be taken to the hospital in Hudson after an accident. Al's been there with the family since early this morning."

"That's awful. Is the teen okay?"

"Looks like it. Apparently, he wrecked the family car and broke a few bones is all. Al said he'll be here in time for the service."

"How can I help?"

She put me to work checking people in, and for the next half an hour, Split City filled with worshipers and conference attendees. I recognized a number of familiar faces among the political types. Most of them had their families with them and appeared happy and relaxed, which was a nice thing to see.

Inside, the TV screens over each scoring table were dark, and our twenty-four lanes stood idle for now. The azure walls and yellow wood of the alley were muted by a brighter light from an open area in front of the restaurant where a podium had been set up and a space had been cleared for a couple of hundred folding chairs. Every seat was taken. Volunteers bustled about, rounding up more chairs for the many others who'd showed up, even moving tables and clearing more space for those who wished to stand.

The service started right on time, with music provided by a couple of singers and guitar players, along with a long-haired fellow playing a drum box. Reverend Al appeared on cue to speak. I'm not much for sermonizing, as a rule, but I thought he did a good job. He kept his message simple and to the point. I didn't pay much attention to the crowd. I figured many of them were just there for the free food and bowling, and indeed, many more conference attendees waited until Jesus Spares was winding down to show up.

#

After the service, the lights around the podium and folding chairs dimmed, the alley lights were turned up, and the screens over the lanes came to life.

Split City had never seen so many people all at once. Things got rolling on our end, and Petula and I and few others spent the next hour giving out free bowling shoes and checking people into time slots for lanes. (The shoes were TreadBos, of course.)

Reverend Al came over to help.

"Nice preaching there, Pastor," I told him.

"Thanks," he said. "But I can't take the credit."

A big, garrulous man with curly red hair and a bushy red beard, Al was a former middle linebacker for the University of Tennessee. He had a welcoming way about him. He also loved to bowl. We'd become friends, so I was okay with him and Petula using our lounge once a week for their Bible study, as well taking over the alley one Sunday a month for the Jesus Spares event.

People located balls to their liking from the racks in back and started bowling. Food and drinks were served in front of our small restaurant on a row of tables manned by more volunteers from the church. Sheriff Lawton was also there with a couple of his deputies keeping an eye on things.

At one point, a pair of state troopers also appeared, and I recognized the governor, no less, coming in through our side entrance. (I found out later Petula had helped to arrange this.) Bo, who'd also arrived toward the end of the church service, headed over to greet the governor.

Cell phones flashed as lots of photos were being taken. One of the media crews had set up also shop with a TV camera and was busy shooting footage.

#

Twenty minutes later, people were happily bowling, eating, or playing video games in our small arcade. Bo, his photo op with the governor over, was clapping and laughing, as he circulated among the rest of the crowd. Things had slowed down enough at the bowling desk that I could consider taking a break.

I was about to do just that when a commotion arose out on the lanes. Apparently, a couple of state legislators, in violation of the weekend rules, had gotten into some sort of policy discussion and dispute. Before long, they started trading insults, along with gutter balls, on adjoining lanes.

Bo, Petula, and I approached them to try to serve as peacemakers. But we were ceremoniously ignored and quickly drowned out by the shouting and finger-pointing.

Things really began to get out of hand, however, a moments later.

The ten-year-old son of the one of the conference goers dropped a twelve-pound bowling ball on the foot of an eight-year-old daughter of a member of an opposing faction.

"Mommy!" The poor little girl began to wail to high heaven.

One father punched the other in the face, and bedlam ensued.

Sides were quickly taken. Kicks, punches, soft drinks, and pizzas flew everywhere. The sheriff and his deputy dove into the mix, attempting to restore order, but they were badly outnumbered.

Onlookers became instant cell phone videographers. (The most trafficked scene on social media turned out to be the governor and his entourage being hastily hustled out the back door by the state troopers.) If that wasn't bad enough, a down-on-his-luck guy from the city—we found out later he had been paid a hundred bucks to appear in a photo op with the governor—urinated on one of our newly refurbished lanes. Which turned out to be a photo op all right.

The media correspondent who'd showed up to try to score an interview with the governor suddenly found herself on the cusp of becoming an overnight internet sensation. Gamely standing in front of the camera with mike in hand as the food flew at the center of it all, she breathlessly intoned: "There seems to be some sort of disagreement taking place here!"

Those weather announcers braving hurricanes never had it so good.

At the height of the bedlam, Bo, Petula, Reverend, and I took up temporary refuge in my office, along with a couple of our employees and a few other members of the church.

Reverend Al and Petula each took chairs, sat down, and closed their eyes.

"What are you doing?" I asked. "Are you okay?"

"Praying," Reverend Al said.

"Good idea."

Those prayers must have had some effect too, because, as it turned out, no one was hurt, thankfully.

The politicians and government officials had marshaled all of their kids, hightailed it to their cars, and cleared out of the area, of course, lest they be caught on camera any more than they already had. The Jesus Spares crowd and the rest of the conference attendees had begun to disperse, since there was obviously no more free bowling or food to be had. By the time more state troopers arrived to reinforce the sheriff, there was nothing they could do—unless we wanted to press charges, which Bo was reluctant to do.

As we emerged from my office to assess the carnage, Bo was stunned into silence. Most everyone else too.

We still didn't know how much all of this was going to cost. (As it would turn out, not even counting TreadBo's huge investment in the weekend conference, Split City had been badly drenched and stained. A couple of our pin setters and lane returns would also need repair in what instantly came to be known on social media as "The Great New York Food Fight.")

"I'm so sorry, Bo," was all I could manage to mutter to my twin brother.

The irony was, the big publicity impact he had been looking for from his weekend conference had actually come to pass. Unfortunately, not in the manner he'd intended.

# 5

Leaving the morgue, I heard my phone ping.

*Billy. Please call me as soon as you can.*

The text was from my ex-girlfriend Justine. Everything with Justine was urgent. Especially when it came to her needs, her priorities, and what she wanted over anybody else.

I had bigger problems at the moment, so I ignored it.

I needed to talk to Bo. The best place to find him right now would be at the factory. Maybe I'd just missed him earlier. He could've been out eating break- fast somewhere. Bo never cooked and hardly ever ate in. Another possibility, knowing Bo, was that he'd been with a woman the night before. If he wasn't at the plant, I'd check back at his condo again.

Partridgeberry was home to around ten thou- sand souls and most of the area's sizeable businesses, including Bo's factory and a small regional printing plant. Nestled in a small valley among the mountains, the town boasted a well-kept main street and village green that fronted on the courthouse. There was also a golf course, a private airport, and a few newer condos scattered among the surrounding hills, Bo's among them.

The TreadBo factory occupied a stylish renovated warehouse next to the railroad tracks on the outskirts of town. No trains ran through the area anymore. But the abandoned, decaying tracks made the factory—with its paved parking lot and adjacent lawn, outdoor kettle drums, wind chimes, crystal formation, state-of-the-art playground, eco-friendly shelter, and picnic tables—appear even hipper.

I managed to squeeze my mud-splattered 4Runner between a Subaru and a rusty oversized van in the nearly full lot. Before climbing out, I took out my phone, opened the browser, and typed in *doppel-gänger*. To my surprise, I discovered that, according to recent research, lookalikes are much more common than most people think.

So, if the dead man was a doppelgänger for Bo and me, what was he doing in Partridgeberry? How did he come into possession of a TreadBo factory access card? And how did he end up dead?

I hadn't visited the factory in a while.

Inside the front door sat Ralph Warrens, TreadBo's wiry seventysomething lobby greeter. He looked up at me in surprise as I walked through the glass front doors.

"I thought you were over in Madaga at the convention." He was busy scribbling something on a piece of paper. "Hold on a sec. My eyesight's not so good anymore. Is that you, Billy? Could've sworn you were Bo there for a second. You guys have to stop doing that to me."

"Hey, Ralph. Bo's away at a convention?"

"Yeah. Some kind of shoe shindig over in Madaga. Didn't he tell you?"

"No." I smiled, sighing in relief. "But it explains a lot."

"What do you mean?"

"Never mind. Bo doesn't always share his social calendar with me."

"Well, that's life in the fast lane for you, I suppose. Your brother's a busy man." He gave me a big wry grin.

"Will you excuse me for a second? Just remembered I have a call to make."

#

Stepping back outside, I found the sheriff's number in my callbacks.

He answered after a couple of rings. "What? Did you forget to tell me something important?"

"No. But I'm over at the TreadBo factory. Bo's not here. They told me he's away, at a shoe convention over in Madaga."

There was silence on the line for a moment.

"All right," the sheriff said finally. "I'll contact the sheriff over there and have them send a couple of deputies to try to find him. Anything else?" He seemed preoccupied.

"What if he calls me back first?"

"Then you should feel relieved," he said and hung up.

\#

"Everything okay?" Ralph asked as I walked back in through the glass door.

"Yeah. I was just hoping to catch up with Bo, but I guess he's not here. Okay if I head upstairs to say hello to Carianne?"

I thought as I long as I was here, I might as well check in with Bo's administrative assistant. Maybe she could shed some light on whatever might have led to the body in the morgue.

"Be my guest," Ralph said with a wink. "Just don't go causing a ruckus. When the folks on the production floor get an eyeful of you through the factory window, they might think Bo's come back to spy on them."

"I'll try to behave myself," I said.

He rose from his desk and, accompanying me to the elevator, pushed the button to open the doors. A paunchy gut spilled over his pants. In another life, Bo'd told me, Ralph had been a top shoe salesman at a men's clothing boutique in the city. But the store had fallen on hard times and gone out of business. Ralph, like a lot of older displaced workers, had fled the city and moved upstate, taking whatever work he could find. Bo said TreadBo was lucky to have him.

Upstairs, the doors opened on the top floor where the management and executive offices were located. A large picture window ran half the length of the hall. It looked down on the factory floor and out toward the back of the building where the shipping department and loading docks were located. The first shift was in full gear with the assembly line running.

Carianne was seated at her desk in her office cubicle outside Bo's office down the hall. She glanced up at me through her glass wall when I stepped out of the elevator.

"Bo?" I heard her say. "What are you—"

"No, Cary, it's me, Billy."

"Billy! Oh, my gosh."

She rose from her chair and came rushing out to greet me. "It's so good to see you. How long has it been?"

"Too long," I said.

She gave me a hug.

I caught a reflection in the glass of her tall frame, long brown curls, blue jeans, and T-shirt. It was standard work attire for TreadBo.

"How have you been?" she asked.

"Great. Looking forward to the summer."

"You look good. But what are you doing here?"

"I stopped by hoping to see Bo."

"Didn't he tell you he was going to be out of town?" Carianne, with a degree in business from the University at Buffalo, had worked for TreadBo for four or five years. Bo told me she could be temperamental but was highly organized. She'd grown up on a dairy farm. Bo joked she was half wholesome and half hip.

"Nope," I said. "I just found out from Ralph downstairs. I saw him a couple of days ago up in Twin Strikes, but he didn't mention it."

"Oh. Well, I'm sure it just slipped his mind. Actually, he only decided to go to the convention at the last minute. He talked to Giuseppe Rhodes and some other people who were headed over there. Addison, our head of marketing, was supposed to represent us at our company booth. But he came down with the flu. So Bo's over there by himself."

I'd heard Bo mention Giuseppe Rhodes a few times. Apparently, he was some hotshot shoe executive from one of TreadBo's larger distributors.

"Is the event at the casino and convention center?" I asked.

"Yeah. The Northeast Shoe Show. Sexy name, right?" She rolled her eyes. "It's kind of a big deal. Schmoozing with store buyers and distributors and the like. We have a small presence every year. It's usually held in New York or Boston or Philadelphia. But for some reason they decided to hold it in Madaga this year. Anyway, at least it's not that far away."

The much larger city of Madaga, located about an hour's drive away, was far more developed than Partridgeberry County.

"Sounds like it wouldn't be Bo's favorite place to be."

"That's for sure. I imagine he's keeping a low profile. You know some people just like to gawk at him because of the name and the quirky shoes."

Carianne was right. In many ways, Bo was the face of TreadBo, the shoe company that bore his name.

"Anyways," she went on, "he's probably holed up working on his laptop in his room whenever he can. I haven't been over to Madaga in a while."

That reminded me. Petula at Split City had told me they'd recently added a new bowling alley to the Madaga casino. I'd been meaning to head over there sometime to check it out. Maybe this would give me a good excuse.

"How long's Bo been up there?"

"Just since yesterday," she said. "The convention started last night. He's due back in a couple of days."

"When was the last time you talked to him?"

"Yesterday afternoon. After he arrived at the hotel. He asked me to email him some product spec sheets first thing this morning for one of the distributors."

"So you haven't talked to him today?"

"No. But I'm sure he'll check in as he usually does. Why?" She looked at me with a troubled expression. "Is something wrong?"

"I just need to talk with him as soon as possible. I've texted him and left a couple of messages but haven't heard back. I know he gets caught up in whatever he's doing and sometimes doesn't respond right away."

"You want me to try to call him too?"

"Yeah, that would be great. Please tell him I'm here and that I need to speak with him right away."

"Sure, Billy." Picking up her phone, she began firing off a text before she'd even finished speaking. "No problem."

I waited while she dialed.

After a minute she said, "I guess he's not answering."

"I guess not," I said. I wanted to tell her more, but now didn't seem like the time.

"If I hear anything from him, I'll be sure to let you know," she said.

I thanked her and turned to leave. But I turned back. "By the way," I asked, "anything unusual happen around here lately?"

"Unusual?" she said with a shrug. "Well, the Split Down the Middle conference catastrophe was certainly unusual. We're still getting calls from reporters. I don't know if we're ever going to hear the end of that."

"Yeah," I said. "You're probably right about that."

I was almost back to the elevator when my phone buzzed in my pocket. I pulled it out, looked at the display, and my heart rate jumped up a few notches.

"Bo?" I asked, feeling like my stomach was about to lurch again.

"Yeah," my brother said.

I broke out in a smile. Looking back at Carianne, I gave her a thumbs-up.

"Oh good. You found him," she said, returning the gesture.

"What going on?" Bo asked. "Carianne was just calling and leaving me a message too. She said you're at my office. And you've been leaving me all of these messages. And the sheriff called me too. Is everything all right at the factory?"

"Yes. Everything's okay here at TreadBo. Hang on a second." I stepped into the stairwell, checked to make sure nobody was there, and lowered my voice so no one else could hear. "Where have you been? Didn't you read any of my texts or listen to my voicemails from earlier?"

He yawned. "Sorry. I've been sleeping, and I guess I must have turned my ringer off. I had a long night, man. I think I had too much to drink. Wow, have I got a splitting headache. I just saw all of these messages and calls."

I started to tell him about what had been going on.

But before I could finish, he interrupted me. "What... Wait a minute. They found a dead body near my office that looks like you and me? What the heck are you talking about?"

"I saw him, Bo. At the morgue here in Partridgeberry. They thought it was you at first. The sheriff asked me to come ID the body."

"You sure you haven't been smoking something, Billy? Wait a sec, I've got another call coming in. It's Sheriff Lawton again."

"That's what I've been trying to tell you. Talk to him, then call me back."

"Okay. Will do."

I breathed out a sigh and felt the tension drain from my shoulders. At least something had finally gone right that morning. Bo seemed alive and well. After he talked to the sheriff, maybe he could begin to help figure out what was going on with the dead guy in the morgue.

I descended the stairs to the first floor and came back out into the lobby, where Ralph was carefully folding a piece of paper.

"Hey, stranger," he said. "That was a short visit."

"Yeah, I know. I just talked to Bo in Madaga."

"Is everything okay?"

"I hope so. He sounded all right."

"Great," he said. "Glad to hear it." He continued folding his piece of paper.

"What are you making there?" I asked.

"A paper airplane for my young granddaughter. She likes me to surprise her with these as little gifts. She has a collection of them, and I'm always trying to come up with new designs."

"That sounds great, Ralph. You must love her very much."

"I do my best," he said with a smile.

# 6

I climbed back into my aging SUV, started the engine, and tried to ignore the fact that, even though it was still chilly, the heater only produced enough warmth to keep me from freezing to death. Bo had dubbed the 4Runner "the dungeon." On the plus side, the "dunge" was edging ever closer to classic status.

As I neared Twin Strikes twenty minutes later, an eagle sailed along the edge of the trees lining the highway. Flush with winter runoff, the river ran muddy and strong on a parallel path below. Approaching Lake Conostowakaka, I caught my first glimpse of our humble little Catskill resort town—dilapidated, yet still managing to glisten from a residue of mist in the noonday sun.

I reached for the dash and turned on the CD player.

"You must be one of the handful of people on the planet who still listens to compact discs," Bo had said to me once. A handful of the silver plastic beauties were, in fact, scattered around the dunge's interior—part of its enduring charm as far as I was concerned. I smiled as James Taylor's "Fire and Rain" poured forth from the aging speakers.

I remembered Justine's text from earlier. Maybe she'd been calling about our dog Hercules. We'd bought the big golden retriever together when we were dating, and I guess you could say we shared custody of the golden retriever, although Herk most often lived with Justine. I speed-dialed her number. The call went to voicemail, so I turned down the music a notch and left her a message.

"Hey, Justine, it's Billy. Just responding to your text from earlier. Call me back when you can."

I passed the town limit's sign—framed by an advertisement for Rick's Used Tires and Auto Repair. There were a few cars in the parking lot at West End Cafe and Creamery, which, many believed, featured the best homemade ice cream in the Catskills. Next, at the first of the town's three traffic signals—blinking yellow this time of year—a Pizza Hut popped into view across the street from an old brick elementary school that had been converted into a nursing home.

Around the next curve, the brown and yellow shape of a patrol cruiser hunkered in its familiar spot in front of the Cumberland Farm's convenience store and gas station. Behind the wheel, I spotted our local sheriff's deputy, Mac Mallen, noshing on a submarine sandwich. I'd known Mallen even longer than I'd known the sheriff, and I slowed to give him a wave. He lowered his window and motioned for me to pull in.

I stopped with my opened window across from his. "Nice lunch."

"Right, huh? It's tofu, beets, avocado, lettuce, tomato, and hot mustard mixed with hemp oil on ancient grain."

"Yummy."

While he was in his late twenties, Mac still had the build of a high school athlete.

"Heard a rumor you were down in Partridgeberry visiting with the sheriff," he said.

"Apparently word travels fast."

"Anything I need to be concerned about?" he asked.

"Why don't I let you talk to the sheriff about that one," I replied, unsure how much he knew.

"Really?" he said, smiling. "After all we've been through?"

"Sheriff Lawton asked me not to talk about it."

"Ooh, Mr. Mysterious. All right. I'm sure I'll find out sooner or later."

First responders always got a free game at Split City, and Mac often took advantage of this perk. When Mac's ball hit the pins, it sounded like a shotgun blast. He had also confided in me once that he'd come from a troubled background. He said he didn't like to dwell on it, but the sheriff had given him a break and helped him turn his life around, which is when he decided to become a deputy.

"When are you going to come by Split City and see us again?" I asked.

"Soon enough," he said. "Anything I can do, you know, to support the local economy. Especially after your little Split Down the Middle fiasco."

"That was Bo's idea."

"Sure, Billy. Whatever you say," he said with a smile.

"I'm touched you care, Mac," I said. I imagined we were destined to be the brunt of local jokes for some time to come.

He laughed, almost choking on a sip of his soft drink, and offered me a peace sign. Mac was allowed to wear his hair long in Native American fashion—though he was about as far from Native American as Black Irish could get. He kept the hair swept back in a dark ponytail that poked out beneath the brim of his sheriff's hat.

"Hey, I think the temperature might actually top fifty degrees today," I said.

"I know." He poked his free hand out the window. "Can you feel it? Keep it real, Billy."

I smiled and gave him a thumbs-up as I raised my window and drove away.

# 7

Outside Split City, I brought the dunge to a stop in the mostly empty lot. It was a far cry from the crowd that had filled the space for the Split Down the Middle Event the month before. A pair of ducks lifted off from the lake, beating their wings as they crossed the road and sailed on overhead.

I climbed out of the truck and looked over the scene. At least it was peaceful. Between our lot and the highway stood The Last Dollar Store and Aubrey's Apple Honey Bakery. I held the latter establishment partly responsible for my recent modest weight gain. Try as I might not to obsess over Aubrey Brown's good looks and winsome personality, I found her pies and cheesecakes impossible to ignore. Petula was always trying to play matchmaker between Aubrey and me. Aubrey, who attended Petula's church, was a few years younger than I. In her early thirties but never married, same as me.

"Well, good morning, Mr. Sunshine. Or should I say good afternoon?" Petula said.

I nodded and returned her greeting as I walked in through the front door.

"What happened to you?" she asked. "You look like you just finished auditioning for an episode of *Ghost Hunters.*"

I didn't want to tell her where I'd been, so I snuck a quick glance at my face in the reflection of the clear glass dome of one of the giant-sized gumball machines we kept next to the counter. My forehead was creased beneath my brown hair, and my face still looked peaked.

"Late night," I lied.

"You have another run-in with Justine or something?"

"No." I shook my head. "Not this time."

"What's going on then?"

"Nothing special."

"Oh, is that right?" she said, folding her arms across her chest with a skeptical furrowing of her brow.

I occasionally developed a nervous tick that caused a tiny muscle between my brow and my ear to twitch. Right now, I imagined that little sucker was quivering away like a tuning fork.

Did I mention Petula was a single mom who'd raised three teens to actual adulthood? Her truth detecting arsenal was nearly beyond compare and would no doubt be circling back to point at me sooner or later—whether I wanted it to or not.

"Oh. I almost forgot." Reaching below the counter, she pulled out a plain white bakery box and set on the counter in front of me. "From our special friend next door."

I knew right away what it was: some kind of a pastry gift from Aubrey.

Petula grinned. "Smells like some piece of heaven. You don't know what kind of will power I've had to exercise all morning to keep from opening that."

I lifted the lid to discover a glazed apple fritter with a gooey maple topping artfully drizzled over its mouthwatering surface. A small card inside read simply THANK YOU. The words were handwritten in Aubrey's flowing yet precise script.

"When are you going to ask that woman out on a date? You know you want to."

"Don't go reading too much into things," I said. "It's just a thank-you present for me jump-starting her car the other morning."

"Aha! Jump-started her car, did you? That's probably not all she's looking to jump-start. If you catch my drift."

"Yeah, I catch it all right. Floors swept and vacuumed?" I asked, changing the subject.

"Yup."

"Ball racks and shoes prepped for the evening?"

"Check," she said.

"Lanes all been oiled?"

"What do you think I've been doing all morning? The most frustrating part of my day."

For those unaware, bowling lanes are oiled daily to protect the wood. It's called "dressing the lane." Like many alleys, we use an automated machine that looks something like one of those robot vacuum cleaners on steroids. Except we purchased ours used, and it can sometimes be temperamental.

"Machine acting up again?"

"Yes," she said. "But I fixed it."

"How did you manage that?"

"I sang to it. And it started working."

"Really," I said. "What song did you sing?"

"A lullaby. The poor thing was just being cranky."

Petula was probably the most efficient person I knew, which lifted a great weight from my shoulders. If that meant singing a lullaby to a lane machine to get it work, so be it.

"Good plan. What about everything else?"

"No problems," she said. "We've had kids descend on the arcade. A few are still in there. Apparently, they're off school today. Some kind of teacher conference or something."

"All right. So, if I'm understanding you correctly, there's absolutely nothing left for me to do."

"Not a thing, boss. Which is why I'm thinking, maybe you and I can take a break, go sit our fannies down on the lawn chairs out back, and smoke a couple of early-afternoon cigars while you tell me all about this late night you just mentioned."

Uh-oh. The last thing I wanted was to be cornered by Petula and have to explain everything about the dead body. Maybe I'd talk to her later when I'd had more of a chance to process things.

"Uh, in case you haven't noticed, it's about to rain," I said, reaching for a distraction.

"What are you talking about?" She craned her neck to look out through the front doors. "Might be a little chilly, but it's beautiful out there."

"Yeah, well, don't forget it's spring, and this is the Catskills. It could start raining at any moment."

"It's not my fault you're so late getting to work. Plus, what's a little rain when you're baring your soul?"

"Maybe later." I turned to make my escape before I revealed too much about the sheriff and the morgue. "I'll be in my office."

"Okay," she said. "But you can't avoid me forever."

I waved to her and started to go.

"Oh, and don't forget," she said over my shoulder, "you've got that exhibition game for the bowlers to-night before league play."

"What?" I stopped and looked back at her. "Again? I thought that was only supposed to be three or four times a year."

"It's been more than four months since your last one."

"It has?"

"Yes. And you barely cracked two hundred the last time. The leaguers weren't impressed."

"Gee, thanks, Petula."

"Just sayin'. Might want to get in a little practice beforehand. I'll be praying for you."

I needed all the prayers I could get. As any pro knows, even the best can sometimes throw a bad game. It takes consistency to crack the top ranks—high score averages over many games and tournaments.

"All right, all right," I said. "I'll try to get in a few practice frames this afternoon. Aren't you having your Bible study here tonight?"

"Not today. Reverend Al had to take his son for some sort of regular checkup at a hospital down south. It's a long trip with the wheelchair van and all. He won't be back for several days."

"Okay."

It would have been nice to have hung out with him this evening. The truth was I still felt a little shaky after what I'd seen this morning. Maybe Petula sensed this in me.

"That's what I mean about the cigar and the talk," she said, smiling. "We've got to get your head back in the game. Oh, and one last thing…Max Fontainebleau stopped by earlier."

"Fontainebleau? What did he want?"

"I don't know. He said something about a potential name change for the resort."

Max Fontainebleau owned the grande dame of Twin Strikes, the historic Conostowakaka Resort, only a short drive outside town. Fontainebleau used to be part owner of an Atlantic City casino. He also happened to be the landlord for our alley, which didn't always put us on the best of terms—not to mention our local representative on the county board of supervisors. He always seemed to be lobbying, directly or indirectly, to bring gambling to Partridgeberry County and in particular to the town of Twin Strikes. Which of course meant at his resort.

"What do you mean a name change?" I asked.

"He said he's not going to change the basic name of the hotel. Just wants to add 'gaming' or something like that to the title. Said he wants to talk with you about it first."

"Figures."

Fontainebleau must have known he was in for a fight with the locals and was probably hoping to marshal my support. If you were a Twin Striker, you were constantly having to spell out the name of the lake and the resort—C-O-N-O-S-T-O-W-A-K-A-K-A—for outsiders. It seemed like every other street or business in the area bore some variant of the lake's moniker. There was Conostowakaka Street, the main drag, of course. Not to mention Conostowakaka

Place, Conostowakaka Court, and Conostowakaka Acres Drive. Then there was Conostowakaka Commons shopping center, Conostowakaka Gardens Apartments, and, well…you get the idea. No one ever considered changing the names of some of the streets to make it easier for tourists, however. Twin Strikers were perversely proud of the lake and resort's nearly indecipherable name.

"I don't trust Fontainebleau," Petula said.

"Me neither."

"Anyway, I asked him if he wanted you to call him about it, but he said no, he would drop by another time. Oh, and Eugene wants to speak with you too. Something about a new pin setting machine."

"I thought you said there were no problems."

"Well, shoot me. I forgot."

"Don't tell me lane six is acting up again."

"No idea," she said. "The man is in his own little world back there. You go deal with him.

# 8

I was heading toward the back of the alley when Bo finally called me back. Glancing back at Petula, I saw she'd disappeared into the front storeroom, so I took a detour and slipped out the back door, closing it behind me.

"Took you long enough," I said.

"Yeah, I talked for a while with Lawton," he said. "I thought you were pulling some kind of a stunt."

"I wish it were."

"Did this guy in the morgue really look like the two of us?"

"Let's just say the sight of a cold corpse that looks freakishly like a pale version of you and me won't be my on my top ten list of life highlights."

"And they think the guy committed suicide," he said. "It's pretty strange. He said the guy even had an office access key card in his pocket."

"Yeah, they showed it to me."

"I still have mine with me. He must have figured out some way to make one."

"Was the extra card registered to you?"

"No. It wasn't registered to anybody," he said. "Weird."

Yeah. Very weird.

"The thought even crossed my mind that he was some sort of separated brother of ours," he said. "An identical triplet like they showed in that documentary. Like we were adopted or something."

He was babbling, clearly nervous.

"Really, Bo? What about our birth certificates and hospital records? Someone would've had to have forged or altered them."

"How do you know? Have you ever seen the hospital records?"

"As a matter of fact, I have. I found them in the files after Mom and Dad passed. It clearly states the birth was identical twins. Nothing about another child, so unless our parents, the hospital, and the doctor are all in on some big conspiracy—which I'd say is pretty unlikely—nobody's going to be making a documentary about us regarding triplets."

He let out a long breath. "All right. Maybe I'm getting a little ahead of myself. I guess the DNA will tell us for sure. I told the sheriff I'd give them a cheek swab to compare against mine. He also said I needed to check on TreadBo's accounts and my personal finances right away in case the guy was trying to pull off some sort of identity theft scam. That's what took me so long to get back to you. I was on the bank's website with my laptop checking the accounts."

"Yeah, I gotta do that too. But I was just going to give them a call. Was everything okay with your accounts?"

"No problems that I can see. There doesn't seem to be any money missing."

"All right. That's a relief. The sheriff thought you'd be the most likely target."

"Still, it's pretty strange, don't you think? This guy going to so much trouble to look like us. And I feel like I'm still waking up, like someone hit more over the head with a brick and this is all some kind of crazy dream."

"Maybe you're just overworked and exhausted. You didn't look so well when I saw you the other day. Sometimes I'm tempted to look up the term *workaholic* in the dictionary. I'm wondering if I might find you name plastered along there beside it."

"Very funny," he said. "But I guess I did sleep for more than twelve hours. After working the convention floor all day, I went to a big party in Pontefio's hospitality suite."

"Was it crowded?" I asked.

"Yeah. There had to be at least fifty people packed in there. They had some good whiskey, and I guess I must've had too much to drink. I shouldn't do that when I'm so tired. All I remember is coming back to my room in kind of a haze and dropping in bed. Didn't even remember turning off my phone."

"Who else was there?"

"A bunch of different people from the convention. Giuseppe Rhodes was in fine form as host."

"Rhodes. Isn't he Pontefio's CEO or something?"

Pontefio was a much bigger, publicly traded company that manufactured and sold a multitude of shoes, including sport shoes.

"Yeah," he said. "He was holding court like some kind of ringmaster. You know, even though he's somewhat of a competitor, Pontefio also acts as distributor for some of our shoes. I felt like I had to stay."

"Well, tell him your twin brother says he's an idiot for letting you get drunk and oversleeping and not answering calls from me and the police."

"Right." He laughed. "Anyway, Lawton is a good sheriff. Hopefully he'll get to the bottom of whoever this guy was. He said they're going talk to some of our staff, and I said that was fine. They're also going to review the security camera recordings and key card access data to make sure the guy didn't get into the building."

"Are you going to check out of the hotel and come back to Partridgeberry?"

There was silence on the line a moment as Bo seemed to hesitate. "The sheriff and I talked about that after I answered some of his questions," he said.

"I don't see any reason to rush back. Everything seems fine from the financial end, and the guy's not coming back to life."

"I'm not sure that's a good idea, Bo."

"Why not?"

"I don't know." I worried something bad was in motion but didn't know why. I stared blankly at the cinder blocked back wall of Split City. "It's just a feeling I have."

"A feeling. Okay. I guess I'd feel the same if I'd had to look at that body the way you did. But I am scheduled to speak on a panel Wednesday. It probably wouldn't look very good if I left in the middle of things and left our booth empty. We've already paid for the convention space, and, after what happened at Split Down the Middle last month, I need to still be a presence."

"Are people talking about it there?" I asked.

"Are you kidding? People can't stop talking about it and asking me questions. I tell you what. How about we sit down over a couple of beers when I get back and we can talk about this dead body then? By then the sheriff should know more."

"I don't know if you're taking this seriously enough, Bo. A guy who looks like us just showed up near your office with his brains blown out."

"I know it's serious. I do. But, like I said, the bank says everything's fine. Nothing's been stolen, and the bank president personally assured me they're putting a close watch on all of our accounts in case anything bad does happen."

I guess when you're the famous Bo Gills, you get to talk directly to the bank president.

"Besides, he was probably just some weird, mentally disturbed person. I don't know," he said.

# 9

Did you know the average bowling ball hits the lane with a pressure of 1,500 pounds per square inch? Eugene Wodka had explained this all to me in great detail more than once.

The G-knome, as we liked to call him, "G" for short, had been part of Split City for decades, long before I set foot in the door. Technically, G was our in-house pin machine mechanic. In reality he was a mad scientist of the kegling game. A pin action guru of the highest order, G arrived early and worked late six days a week. Every day except Sundays, when he attended mass and visited his elderly mother, who lived in an assisted care facility in the area.

This afternoon I found him in his usual spot hovering over his worktable behind one of the pin setter mechanisms, fussing over a circuit board. An ex-Marine and former journeyman on the pro tour, G practically sweated lane oil.

"What's wrong, G?"

"What's wrong?" He didn't look up. "I'll tell you what's wrong. Like I been trying to tell you people, ever since you guys stuck your foot in it with that big stunt you pulled last month, these machines ain't been right. Now I gotta replace this whole dang mechanism. Unless you can pull some magic out of those TreadBos of yours."

I shifted my shoulders and took a deep breath. "Remember, that whole weekend was TreadBo's idea," I said, calmly throwing Bo and his marketing director under the bus for the hundredth time.

"Yeah, sure," he said. "Whenever I'm feeling too happy and want a good cry, I can still pull out my phone to watch some of the videos."

Here in the continued aftermath of the debacle, I clapped my chief bowling scientist on the shoulder. "I'm sorry. That was a colossal screwup all right. I really do understand how it's made your job more difficult."

"You think?" G said with a smirk. "Whatever happened to law and order?"

I let go of his shoulder.

"And what am I going to do about the mess of this machine?" he asked.

"You know we can't afford any new equipment right now. Our property insurance company says their underwriters are still investigating. Not sure if they'll cover anything or not. Apparently, they've never seen anything like this before."

"Well, duh. None of us have seen anything like that before." He shook his head and sighed.

"Look, I don't have to tell you, you're a genius when it comes to fixing this equipment. There's no one I would trust more than Eugene Wodka when it comes to keeping the heartbeat of this old alley alive."

"Uh-huh." G shifted the toothpick from one side of his mouth to the other. "Very poetic, Billy."

"No, I'm serious. When you go, Split City goes with you."

"I doubt it," he said. "Now get the heck out of here and leave me alone so I can finish my work."

#

Around 6:30 that evening, my head was beginning to nod over a financial spreadsheet in my office. Petula worked the desk as a handful of league bowlers warmed up out on the lanes. It was almost time for me to begin warming up before my exhibition game. Distracted by my talk with G and a few other issues that had cropped up, there'd been no time for practice.

I looked up to see a smiling Aubrey Brown darkening my open door.

"I brought you something." She held out a plate with a turkey sandwich and a couple of freshly baked chocolate chip cookies I could smell from across the room.

In that moment she looked like one of prettiest sights I'd ever seen. Dark jeans nicely framing her willowy figure. Her long auburn hair gathered up into a low bun. How she preserved her physique around all of the sumptuous fare her bakery churned out was a mystery to me. I'd met her teen son, Kyle, a few times—a respectful, shy young man with a tinge of sadness about him. Her late husband had died when the boy was only seven.

My mouth began to water. "Those cookies can't be for me. Take 'em to G. He's the skinny one around here."

She put her hand on her hip, smiled, and offered me a fake look of disappointment.

"Kidding of course. They get anywhere near that old man, they'll be gone faster than summer snow."

She laughed.

"But seriously," I said. "Thank you. You shouldn't have."

"Oh, it's nothing," she said. "I thought you might be hungry. Petula said you looked tired and distracted."

"Oh, she did, huh?" I smiled.

"Is everything okay?" she asked.

"Yeah. Just having a really long day, that's all."

Which was true, as far as it went. And all I had to look forward to at home was a frozen pizza and a bottle or two of beer.

"She's right though." She appraised me with a quizzical look. "You don't seem yourself."

"Maybe it's my advancing age."

"Hah. You and me both. You're turning forty in a couple of years, aren't you?"

"Don't remind me."

"We'll have to celebrate. I used to think forty sounded old. But it doesn't anymore."

"You're right about that." I couldn't help but appreciate how comfortable she was to be around. Was it just my imagination?

"Well, I won't keep you." She stepped into the room and placed the food on the edge my desk. "I hear you're about to do some bowling."

"Yeah. Don't remind me. Exhibition. Just hope I don't embarrass myself."

"Oh, you'll be great. No matter what." She flashed a grin. "I'd stay to watch with Petula, but I have to go pick up Kyle and get him some dinner."

"Of course. Thanks again."

"You're welcome." And with that she was gone, just as quickly as she'd come.

*Strange*, I thought, *how people come together sometimes. How kindness can appear when you least expect it.* I didn't understand it then, but after the weird shock of seeing the body that morning, I was in desperate need of such a kindness.

I turned off my computer, slipped on my bowling shoes, and went to work on the turkey sandwich.

# 10

I sat still in my office chair with my eyes closed. Visualizing the swing of my arm, the release of the ball, strikes and spares. It was a pregame ritual I'd practiced ever since I began bowling professionally. Generally speaking, the better my pregame visualization of desired results, the better I bowled.

But it was not going to happen this evening. My phone began to buzz on my desk. I ignored it the first time, but it began to buzz again.

I sighed, opened my eyes, and picked up the phone. Sheriff Lawton.

*What now?*

"I'd like to meet with you again," he said when I answered. "I have a few more questions."

"When?"

"Now. I'm in Twin Strikes."

"Right now? I'm supposed to bowl an exhibition game in half an hour."

"This shouldn't take long," he said.

*Great.*

After making a lame excuse to Petula, I headed out the front door, telling her I'd be back in time to bowl.

#

In the Denny's down the street from Split City, the sheriff stirred a packet of sugar into his coffee. I sat opposite him in a booth. Our corner of the restaurant was empty.

"I know you're pressed for time," he said.

"I'm just glad it isn't Bo lying down there in the morgue."

"Me too. But I'll feel a whole lot better when I've got a better handle on what's happening here."

"This dead guy must have been some kind of a lookalike imposter."

"I suppose. We'll see." He took a sip of his coffee, then put the mug back down. He still seemed to be eyeing me with suspicion, and I had no idea why. It seemed like there were things he wasn't telling me. But he didn't seem at all uncomfortable. Maybe dead bodies in the morning had been routine for him back when he was a city cop.

"You think he was after money?" I asked.

"Could be," he said.

"Maybe something else is going on. I checked my bank accounts and credit, and everything looks fine. Bo said the same for him."

"Yeah, that's what he's told me."

"It's all very strange," I said.

It was growing dark outside. I looked out the window at a large piece of farm equipment someone was driving down the street.

"When do you think you will have more of an idea about who the dead guy is?" I asked.

"Soon enough, I hope."

He said he was still waiting for the medical examiner's report to arrive. The man, a private general practitioner who only served as ME part time, had been out fly fishing somewhere the past couple of days.

As he finished speaking, a heavyset man who reminded me of William Conrad on the old TV private detective series entered the diner and made a beeline for our table. The sheriff introduced him as Deputy Leonard Scriblow, then made room for Scriblow to sit down next to him.

"Lenny does investigative work for me," the sheriff said. "He's the one who took the call and was first on the scene with the body."

"I was sorry about your brother," Scriblow said to me. "I was sure it was him. After all, I've seen Bo Gills around town plenty of times. All those people having jobs in the factory, cranking out those crazy shoes of his. Been great for the county. Shame what happened here in Twin Strikes with that conference of yours. Hope it doesn't damage your brother's business."

There was a pause for moment while the sheriff looked around as if to make sure no one else was listening. "Okay, Billy," he said. "I'm going to level with you about something. There's a reason we wanted to come up here to meet with you. Our dead guy in the morgue? We don't think this is a suicide."

It took a moment for his words to sink in.

"You think someone killed him?" I whispered.

"It's looks that way. And with all of the craziness that's been going on around here, people from out of town and what not…we need to ask you a few more questions."

"Sure. I mean, of course," I said, suddenly feeling defensive.

Scriblow produced a little notebook from his pocket, apparently preparing to take notes. He also pulled out his smartphone and slid it halfway across the table toward me. "You mind if I record our conversation?"

"Should I be talking to a lawyer?" I asked.

"No need for that." The sheriff motioned to his deputy. "Lenny, shut that thing off."

Scriblow didn't look happy about the situation but did as he was told.

The sheriff turned back to me. "Now. How often do you and your brother talk?"

"Talk? I don't know how often," I said. "It's not like I keep a log of our conversations."

"Wouldn't you say you and your brother are close. Being twins and all?"

"Not really," I said. "It doesn't always work like that. We might talk once a week. Sometimes more or less. But when he's busy working or going off on one of his crazy adventure trips, I hardly hear from him."

"Doesn't he own the bowling alley with you?"

"Yeah. But he's never here. I mean, except for the conference last month."

"Has he seemed depressed of late?"

I got the strange feeling this situation was beginning to spin out of control. The sheriff seemed to be on to something about Bo, and he was probing me for answers about it.

"No. Well, maybe a little. Especially after what happened last month."

"Is he having money problems?"

"He said money's tight right now for TreadBo. He's got a big payroll and all, so I guess you could say he's under some stress with that. But, you know, Bo's earned a lot in the past. He's always been more careful with money than I have. He's pretty obsessive it."

"Obsessive, huh?" Scriblow interrupted, furiously writing down notes.

"No," I said. "I didn't mean—"

"Ok, we get it." The sheriff held up his hand. "How's the bowling alley doing? Times are tough. Being a small business, you must be under some money pressures yourself from time to time."

"Am I under investigation here or something?"

"No," he said. "I was just curious."

"I'm not under any more money pressure than what I'm used to," I said. "Like most everything else around here, our business is pretty seasonal. We rock and roll in the summer, have our ups and downs for the rest of the year. I manage to provide my few workers a steady paycheck. Myself most of the time, too."

"Mmm… How much do you actually know about TreadBo and the company's finances?"

I had to think about that for a second. "To be honest, not much. Like I told you, Bo and I own Split City together, but he's basically a passive investor. And he doesn't talk to me much about the factory or TreadBo's finances."

"Interesting." The sheriff wrote down something in his own notebook, then closed the cover. "All right. I think that about covers it for now."

He motioned to Scriblow to go pay the bill. The elder man exited the booth, and that uneasy feeling crept over me again.

"If you don't mind me saying so, Sheriff," I said, "seems like you suspect Bo might have gotten mixed up in something."

"I didn't say that."

"Shouldn't you be more focused on the guy who was murdered?"

"Don't worry. We're very focused."

That sounded ominous.

"Are you through with me?" I asked. "I need to go bowl an exhibition game."

"Yes. But keep your phone handy. We may need to talk to you again or bring you over to the station for further questioning."

# 11

Later, exhausted, I struggled to keep my eyes open as I drove up the driveway to my cabin.

The cedar-and-glass dwelling wasn't much, but it suited me well. Only a five-minute drive from Split City, the two-bedroom A-frame stood atop a hill overlooking the lake. With only a few years left on the mortgage, the place had become home.

Tired as I was, I felt uneasy. I was puzzling about my being questioned again by the sheriff and stewing about the bowling slump I was in.

That's when I noticed Justine standing in the driveway within the glow from my front deck light, her arms folded across her chest. She was leaning against the hood of her arctic-white Jaguar SUV. Her platinum-blonde hair framed the Greta Garbo pout I'd once found adorable but now avoided.

"Shoot," I said to myself, remembering.

With everything else that had been going on, I'd completely forgotten she was coming by to drop off Herk for me to watch while she was away at a conference.

"You're very late," she said, fixing me with a look I'd seen a thousand times before as I extracted myself from the dunge.

"I apologize."

"Didn't you get any of my texts?"

"I got one text, yes. And I texted you back."

Her mouth flatlined. "And then I texted you back again. Twice. To remind you I was bringing Herk."

"You did?" I pulled out my phone. Sure enough, two more texts from Justine appeared on the screen. I hadn't pulled my phone out to look at it since I'd started bowling earlier. The texts had been sent a couple of hours before.

"You just forgot I was coming today, didn't you, Billy?"

"Yes," I admitted. "I'm sorry. I had my phone on silent and forgot to turn it back on."

"That's a lot of forgetting," she harrumphed, her green eyes attempting to cruise-missile my soul. "I told you I had to leave tonight for my conference." She and Sheriff Lawton could have had a stare-off competition.

"You're right. I messed up. I should have been here to meet you like I told you I would."

A successful corporate attorney who commuted to Westchester County each day, Justine was also an expert fly fisherwoman and downhill skier. She was pretty darn wonderful at just about everything else she did as well. Petula called her the "intimidator." What she'd ever seen in me, a washed-up bowler with what some might call a still modestly handsome appearance, I hadn't a clue.

She continued to glare at me. Her failure to acknowledge my apologies for my mistakes, not to mention her my-way-or-the-highway demeanor, had eventually driven us apart. That and the fact I'd discovered that she'd been cheating on me via an ongoing, long-term affair with one of her firm's married partners—for which she'd never apologized of course.

"Right. You messed up again. That's no excuse," she said. Years of yoga, spiritual retreats, and mindfulness exercises seemed to be doing battle within her against the urge to go Mt. Vesuvius on me for the umpteenth time.

Trying to see beyond the potential blast, I glanced over her shoulder at Herk, who was patiently staring out at us from the back window of the Jag.

"Fine," she said at last, shaking her head and rolling her eyes as if I were little more than a bothersome thorn in her flesh. "Let's just get Herk inside and settled so I can be on my way."

Yoga 1. Vesuvius 0. Not that my attempt at an apology was in any way deserving of a Nobel Peace Prize.

She turned to open the car door for Herk, who leaped out and raced over to greet me with his brown eyes sparkling and tongue hanging out. I bent down and was practically knocked over by the big beast as he stood on his hind legs slobbering me with licks. "Hey, buddy. I missed you too," I spluttered, balancing his front paws against my chest.

"There's our baby boy." Justine suddenly beamed with genuine affection—not at me but at the dog. Herk's tail swished back and forth like an out-of-control feather duster.

"Maybe he needs a pet psychologist to train him not to jump up on people," I said.

"Maybe you should be the one doing the training," she countered.

"That's all right. I don't mind him jumping on me. See, he already forgives me for forgetting you were coming. Don't you, Herk?"

"Yes, but he's a dog, and sometimes dogs can be enablers."

As usual, she had a quick answer for everything.

It was pointless to argue with her. The dry air was growing colder, and the last thing I needed right now was more of a lecture. I spun around and headed for the deck and sliding glass door. Justine followed with Herk trailing along between us as though we were still a happily dating couple.

I unlocked the door, and they followed me into the cabin's main living area.

"It's cold in here," Justine said.

Without moving to do anything about it, I replied, "Yeah. I'll have to turn up the heat."

"And something smells awful. Phew. You should get a cleaning person in."

Like I could afford that.

She immediately began to examine the evidence of my hasty departure from that morning. Dishes left piled in the sink. A faucet still dripping. A half-eaten pile of scrambled eggs with bacon on a plate. There was a fry pan on the counter and the charred remains of two pieces of raisin bread, which I'd been in the middle of toasting when the sheriff called.

"You're not usually this much of a slob, Billy."

"Sorry. I was in a hurry when I left this morning."

Her face flashed impatience as she got a closer look at me.

"What's wrong with you?" she asked.

"Nothing."

"Really?"

"I just bowled a bad exhibition game in front of the league bowlers."

"That's all?" she asked, fixing me with a lawyerly stare.

I nodded. I wasn't about to go into the whole story about the dead body with her.

Plus, it was entirely true that I'd barely scratched out a modest score of 178 in front of my evening audience. The leaguers didn't care that I'd been called to the morgue early that morning. They wanted to see a pro bowler in action. Virtually all of them had stopped watching before the final frame. Only Petula stayed, with a pained expression on her face. "Go home. Get some sleep. I'll close," was all she'd said.

Herk splayed out on the cabin floor where he'd lain a hundred times before, a canine bridge over troubled waters.

A burst of wind blew up the from the lake and vibrated the windowsills. The Pennsylvania round face grandfather clock Justine had given me as a birthday present a couple of years before still ticked away in the corner. On the wall next to my recliner hung a photo of my mother and father standing arm in arm with Bo and me when we were kids. The picture was taken on a beach somewhere. I was pretty sure it was Cape Cod. There used to be photos of Justine and me on the wall too, and a few photos of Justine when she was younger. But I'd taken those down and put them in a box in the basement.

"You have enough food and treats for our guy?" she asked. "Because, if you don't, I've got more in the car."

"Got it all covered, Mama Bear. And"—I paused for dramatic effect as I reached into the drawer of the lamp table next to the couch—"I just so happen to have Mr. Hercules' favorite toy handy."

Out came the elongated rubber ducky from its resting place. It wheezed a sharp squeak as I gave it a squeeze. Herk jumped to his feet with a bark. I made him work for it. He had to sit, lie down, and roll over. Then I tossed it on the floor, and he was off to the races, attacking the poor hapless creature like he could never get enough.

"All right, well, I've gotta hit the road." Justine looked at her watch. "My flight leaves early in the morning from LaGuardia, and I have a three-hour drive ahead of me." She knelt down over Herk and scratched his ear. "Don't worry, puppy. Mommy will be back on Friday."

She turned toward me, and as she did, I caught a hint of her favorite body lotion, a scent that reminded me of the not-so-subtle seduction she'd used so effectively on me a few years before. Beneath her expensive open topcoat, she was clad in an outfit that seemed perfectly apportioned to her long legs, attractively accentuated by a black blazer dress and bright-white blouse. The dress seemed a tad too short. Her heels a tad too high.

I looked away and tried not to make eye contact. Which, when I finally did glance her way, wasn't all that hard because she seemed bent on giving me her patented cold-eyed stare. She'd conditioned me to look through her and beyond her whenever she resorted to such a tactic, which only infuriated her all the more.

"And don't forget to give our big boy here lots of love and attention while I'm gone," she said.

"No problem there," I said.

Herk dropped his toy on the floor in front of me, waiting for me to toss it to him again.

"Oh, you want to play, do you?" I said to Herk.

A moment later, I glanced her way as she was heading out the door, saying, "See you in a couple of days," over her shoulder. Then she disappeared, leaving the sliding door part way open.

I sat down with Herk's toy in my hand in the living room chair, listening to her heels crunch across the driveway, her car door shut with a heavy thud, and its engine roar to life. Herk nuzzled at my hands and the toy. I scratched his ear and patted his head, still listening as the sound of her tires rolling over gravel echoed through the surrounding woods until it could no longer be heard, relieved she was gone.

I tossed the toy at my feet for Herk to gnaw on, rose, and went to close the door.

Then I kicked off my boots and sat down, going back in my mind through the experience at the morgue. Maybe the guy I'd been called in to ID was just some nut lookalike with a shoe fetish or whatever, but that didn't seem to ring true. My gut told me something more sinister was going on, which, on top of having to deal with Justine again, left me feeling like I was back in high school or bowling as rookie on the tour.

Herk trotted over and lay patiently at my feet, his nose poking out so it was almost touching one of my toes.

"Hey, buddy," I said. "I'm really glad you're here. Maybe we can be partners over the next couple of days.

He leaned in closer and rested his big head against my foot.

"That's my dog."

I suppose I slept some that night, although I was hardly aware of it. Herk lay in his usual spot on the rug next to the bed. I awoke once in the middle of the night to hear him whimpering and moaning in his sleep, dreaming doggie dreams.

# 12

I awoke in the gray light of early dawn. Glancing out the window, I spied a coating of dew on the ground. The sight made me restless. Maybe because the thought of a dead body that looked like me still percolated in my mind.

Normally, I loved taking Herk to work with me. He was a joyful spirit who greeted bowlers when they walked in the door at Split City, and most of them seemed to like it too. Petula even kept a bag of doggie snacks with Herk's name on it in a drawer behind the counter.

But this morning was different. Reaching for my phone to check the forecast, I learned the temperature was predicted to rise into the fifties.

"What do you say, buddy?" I said to Herk. "How about a quick hike up the mountain?"

His tail start thumping wildly on the rug below the bed before I'd even begun to move.

#

After coffee and a quick breakfast, we left the cabin, winding our way our way down to the lake and onto the rough trail that, in this sparsely developed area, circled the water. Overnight cold still hung in the air, but a promising sun was bursting over top of the mountains to light up the sky. I tossed a stick for Herk to retrieve, and he leaped into action.

After I tired of throwing the stick, Herk ran on ahead to clear the way of any offending geese who might decide to lay their daily defecation in our path. He soon spotted a couple on the trail, charged at them, and sent them flying off with loud honking complaints over the lake. I didn't know what the big retriever would ever do if, by some chance, he ever happened to catch a goose.

Reaching the end of the lake, we turned and spent the rest of the morning meandering up the switchback spruce trail that climbed the mountain. I was reminded once again how I'd always felt at home in the woods.

#

I called Petula late that morning.

"Sleep in late again?" she said after picking up her phone.

"I just felt like I needed a little time off."

"Lucky you, Mr. Former Big Time Bowler."

Ouch. I explained how I'd forgotten Justine was bringing Herk last night and told Petula where we were.

"No explanation needed, Chief," she said. "After the way you bowled in front of those leaguers last night, I figured you might need some time to clear your head."

"It was that bad, huh?"

"I hate to say it, but you need to get your act together. I know that Split Down the Middle disaster was a tough thing to have happen. But…"

Little did she know. I'd heard nothing more from Sheriff Lawton. Nothing from Bo at the convention in Madaga either. The silence left me feeling strange. I was also feeling tired after my early rising and the hike, so I decided to sit out on the front porch in one of the rockers to see if I could take a power nap before lunch.

Herk lay at my feet, his head resting between his outstretched paws. The sun's rays warmed my legs as I watched a pair of geese floating serenely across the water at the edge of the lake below. Normally, I might have fallen asleep. But I couldn't escape the gnawing feeling that something was deeply wrong.

Then I remembered how the sheriff had been so focused on TreadBo. It stood to reason that whatever had brought the dead man to where his body was discovered had something to do with the factory and the company.

I decided to give the sheriff a call to see how the investigation was going. Just as I was fishing the phone from my jacket pocket, it began to ring.

I looked at the screen. Wouldn't you know.

I answered it. "You've got to stop waking me up like this." Mr. Smart Alec.

"It's coming on to noon," the sheriff said.

"I know. But after yesterday I was thinking about taking a nap."

"Oh yeah? How's that working out for you?" He sounded like he never slept, let alone took a nap.

"It isn't, actually. I was just about to call you to find out where things stood with the investigation."

"I have a couple more questions for you." He paused. "Have you talked with your brother any more since yesterday?"

Herk stirred at my feet as I sat up a taller in the rocker. "No."

"When did you last talk to him?"

"Yesterday afternoon."

"I assume you two had some further discussion regarding the body in the morgue."

"Of course. It's a big deal. Or at least I think it is."

"How did you leave it with him?"

What was the sheriff driving at? I sensed something different in his voice, a unique kind of urgency that hadn't been there the day before. I felt a chill form in my stomach as the dull anxiety I'd been feeling seemed to come into sharper focus. Part of me wanted to be as forthcoming as possible. Another part warned me to be cautious. So I hedged.

"He said he thought the dead man was some crazy lookalike."

"But did he seem concerned about it?"

"Well, yeah, of course. Wouldn't you be?"

I didn't like where this conversation was heading.

"But he's still in Madaga," I added. "He's scheduled to speak on a panel. I don't know… Maybe he figures the lookalike guy is just part of the cost of his keeping his name and his company in the public eye."

I guessed none of this would have been new information to the sheriff.

"Did Bo say anything else about the dead man?" he asked.

"No. Why? Is something wrong?"

"I can't get into that right now."

"What? Why not?"

"You'll find out soon enough. Just go to work at your alley, do whatever it is that you do. We will probably need you to come back over here later today or tomorrow to answer a few more questions."

"Can't you tell me anything?"

"Not right now, Billy. I've got to go. I'll be in touch."

I started to say something else, but he'd already hung up.

I sat still for a moment, looking out over the lake. What was going on? Instead of making me feel better, the sheriff's call had only ratcheted up my anxiety. I pushed up from the rocking chair and left it swaying. Stepping back inside, I grabbed my keys and coat from the peg by the front door. I reversed course, exited, and locked the door. The storm door banged behind me as Herk rose to his feet, shook himself, and began to trot along beside me.

"Come on, my friend," I said. "Let's take a ride."

# 13

It was the middle of the lunch hour by the time I made it to the TreadBo factory in Partridgeberry. What I didn't expect to find there were a couple of sheriff's department vehicles in front of the building, along with Scriblow and another deputy carrying boxes out the front door. I spotted Sheriff Lawton behind the wheel of his idling cruiser at the edge of the lot and went over to him. He powered down his window.

"What's going on?" I asked.

"I might ask you the same thing. I thought you were going to work at the alley."

"C'mon, Sheriff. You can hardly expect me to sit still after what you told me on the phone. Or what you didn't tell me, that is."

He sighed. "We've served a warrant and are searching the building."

"Oh good," I said. "I was afraid you might be setting up a speed trap for hot-rodding late-shift workers."

"Very funny." He didn't look amused.

"So this is definitely a murder investigation." I crossed my arms.

"No comment."

"Can I go inside?" I had no idea what I might be looking for, but obviously my thinking was running along the same lines as the sheriff when it came to TreadBo.

"Not right now." The door locks clicked open, and he gestured. "Why don't you climb in front here and let's have a chat?"

It sounded more like a command than a question, so I hesitated. Then I went around, opened the passenger door, and climbed in.

The sheriff's car was outfitted with a laptop computer, a radio, and some other high-tech-looking gear. A steel mesh barrier and thick glass separated the front seats from the back. I glanced over my shoulder, thankful to be in the front.

The sheriff turned to look at me. "Comfy?"

"Is Bo in some trouble?"

"I hope not. This search is standard procedure."

*Standard procedure.*

Wonderful. Then why did it feel like something more?

"What I want to know," he continued, "is why you are really here."

"I drove all the way down here because I'm still concerned about identity theft or something worse happening with my brother. Can't you give me a little more of an idea of what's going on?"

His look gave nothing away.

I waited.

"All right," he said. "I'm going to give you some information I shouldn't give you, but don't expect much more." He hesitated. "We ran the corpse's fingerprints through the national and international criminal database again after we were able to pull a partial print. Looks like our dead man was trying to alter his prints or make them untraceable using some sort of burning solution, but he wasn't fully successful."

"Okay. Wow. Why would he do something like that?"

"Because that's what some criminals do. The dead man's name was Etienne Bouchard. He was Canadian. From Quebec. And he had a long rap sheet. Assault and battery, grand larceny, plus four counts of embezzlement, along with failure to pay child support, just to name a few of his convictions."

"That doesn't sound good. Why wasn't he in prison?"

"With the Canadian penal system being a bit less, shall we say, penal than our own, Bouchard managed to skate when it came to doing any serious jail time. Barely served three months on the grand larceny and assault before being moved to a halfway house. His old mug shots showed that he bore quite a striking resemblance to you and your brother, too."

I shook my head to clear it. Everything seemed to be happening so fast. "But what was he doing in Partridgeberry, and why would someone kill him?"

"That's why we're here." He stared at me with a blank face. "I just talked to a Canadian Mountie. In recent years, he said, Bouchard was working as a chef in a small-town restaurant. But apparently, he's also developed some pretty advanced computer hacking skills on the side. And he's been suspected in a number of cybercrimes."

"Are you imagining Bouchard had a partner?" I asked, probably liking this sleuthing a little more than was good for me.

"I don't imagine things," he said. "I follow the evidence."

"I'm guessing you haven't located Bouchard's car, if that's how he got to Partridgeberry. Because if you had, you might've known sooner who he was."

The sheriff shook his head. "What are you now, a detective? For your information, no. We haven't located any car. But we did find some cracked glass and plastic not far from where the body was found. We're getting it analyzed to see if we can figure out where it came from. It looks like two vehicles may have crashed into one another."

"Does Bo know you're here searching his factory?" I asked.

"Yes, your brother knows we're here."

"What does he have to say about it?"

"That's all I'm going to tell you." The sheriff paused, glancing toward the building. "Because you're a friend, and I don't want to start considering you a material witness or a suspect."

What was that supposed to mean? He obviously wasn't giving me the whole story. Nor would I have expected him to.

I gazed out across the parking lot as I thought about what he'd told me. I could only imagine how the TreadBo employees must have been feeling about all of this. The shadow of a cloud was moving slowly over the building.

"Just stay out of our way, Billy. Go back over to Twin Strikes and go to work," he said. "It'll be better for everyone if you do."

"I don't get it," I said.

"I don't expect you to."

The pause was long enough to make me feel uncomfortable. But what more could I do? I was out of options.

#

On the way back to Twin Strikes, I wrestled with the possibilities. The sheriff had probably already told me more than he was supposed to. But why was he being so cryptic?

As far as I knew, I had nothing to hide. And neither did Bo.

But then again, like I've been saying, my brother and I weren't exactly close. How much could I have known?

I double-checked the time and dialed Bo's phone. The call started to ring, but, like the morning before, my brother didn't answer. This time the call went immediately to voicemail.

"It's me," I said. "Call me back as soon as you get this message. It's extremely urgent."

I pulled the car to the side of the road and sent him a text message as well before continuing on.

An hour passed with no response. Time enough for me to make it back to the cabin, grab a bite to eat, and get ready to head to the alley.

When I finally did hear back from Bo, his text was as cryptic as the sheriff's words had been—but far more shocking.

*TWO STATE TROOPERS JUST SHOWED UP. THEY'RE TAKING ME TO MADAGA BARRACKS. "2 ANSWER MORE QUESTIONS." THE SHERIFF ALSO CALLED. HE SAID THEY'VE SERVED A WARRANT AND THEY'RE IN THE PROCESS OF SEARCHING THE FACTORY. CAN YOU TELL ME WHAT'S GOING ON?*

I immediately texted back, *I DON'T KNOW*, and waited.

But I received no text back.

According to the GPS on my phone, it would take more than an hour to drive to the state trooper barracks in Madaga. I snatched up my keys, a protein bar, and bottle of water from the pantry. Then I took Herk's leash from its peg on the wall, bent down, and clipped it to his collar.

"Up for another adventure?" I asked the big dog.

He barked his agreement, and we were out the door once again.

# 14

Traffic, mostly for the casino no doubt, was beginning to build by the time I arrived in Madaga. I counted license plates from Vermont, New Jersey, and Connecticut, and from as far away as North Carolina.

When it came to resort towns, the big M made our humble burg of Twin Strikes look like little more than an unsightly pimple on a map. A lot had changed since the time I'd first visited Madaga more than a decade before. A huge road sign filled with colorful images of wildlife, the casino, and the mountains shouted out a welcome at the town entrance. What had once been a quiet main street had morphed into a wide avenue complete with turn lanes, attractive median trees, and planters flanked by dozens of newer structures. People, restaurants, and parking lots seemed to be everywhere, and shops sold everything from maple syrup and Catskill crafts to tourist trinkets and cheap beer.

Backing it all, of course, the Great Madaga Casino, Hotel, and Convention Center —owned and operated under special state license by the Native American Madaga tribe—poked up like some postmodern glass-and-granite cathedral, fourteen stories tall.

The building that housed the state trooper barracks—a single-story edifice with a gray stone facade and narrow windows framing a reinforced glass entrance—was located on the east end of town. Turning into the lot, I immediately spotted Bo's Range Rover parked in front, along with a couple of other cars.

Heaps of plowed snow still ringed the lot, melting in the afternoon sun. I let Herk out and took him for a brief walk in a brown patch of grass between the building and a parking lot next door. I gave him some water, then left him in the dunge with a big rawhide to chew and one of the windows open a crack.

The front of the barracks building was flanked by boxwoods protected against the deep winter snows by little teepee-like triangles made of wood.

Behind a counter inside the entrance sat a large woman in a short-sleeved uniform with a badge pinned to her ample chest. "How'd you get past me?" she said, her gaze shooting switchblades in my direction as I entered. "You're supposed to be staying in the room where the deputies took you until Sheriff Lawton shows up."

"What? I'm—"

"Are you looking for a bathroom? You think we use outhouses around here?"

"I think you have me confused with someone else," I finally said.

"Hold on a second." She rose from behind the counter. Round face, dark hair, and biceps to rival any weightlifter. Complete with Patton-style pearl-handled .45 caliber sidearm.

It was hard not to stare.

She moved around the counter to get a closer look at me, advancing toward me like a prowling mother bear. "Aren't you the guy we just put in back to wait? Aren't you, Mr. Gills?" She was nearly my height and had to weigh more than two hundred pounds, most of which appeared to be solid muscle.

"Nope," I said. "I'm not the man you're looking for. But I am his brother."

"Say what?" She squinted.

"Yes. I'm Billy Gills, Bo's brother."

"Oh, all right." She made a long face. "Name's Maracle. I'm station commander here."

As I was soon to learn, Trooper Sergeant Bluewind Maracle was one part Iroquois, one part Asian, and, at least on the surface, one hundred percent pissed off much of the time. She could outshoot, out manhandle, and outrun most other state troopers.

"You guys twins or something?" she asked, giving me a more thorough look over.

"That's right."

"Wait, wait, wait…" She tilted her head as she continued to look at me. "You've got to be kidding me!" As if she'd been struck by lightning, her face lit up in a huge smile that might've even been charming. "Holy Hollywood. When they brought your brother in, I didn't make the connection."

"What connection?"

"I know you guys. I know who you are. He's Bo Gills, the bowler and creator of TreadBo shoes. And you're Billy Gills. You run that little bowling alley up in Twin Strikes."

"Split City Lanes."

"Yeah, that's it." She was suddenly beaming. "I can't believe it."

"What do you mean?" I had no idea what she was talking about. I'd never seen her before in my life.

"You guys were the Twin Terrors of Ticonderoga. Right here in my department. I gotta tell you, Mr. Gills, I'm a longtime fan." She stuck out her meaty paw and pumped my hand.

Good thing Sergeant Maracle hadn't seen me bowl a stinker of a game in front of all of the league bowlers the night before.

"You know, I followed you guys for years," she went on. "I was trying to get good enough to go pro myself. Until I discovered my true calling."

"You mean being a state trooper."

"No, fool. Women's professional wrestling. Bigga Mama Whompa, at your service." She gave a little bow.

"Always honored to meet a fan." Which was the absolute truth. They were growing more and more rare. "Thank you."

"No, Mr. Gills. Thank *you*. Believe it or not, I was there in Vegas the day you and Bo bowled matching three hundred games. It was incredible. No one had ever seen anything like it. Double perfection. Should have been on the cover of *Sports Illustrated* if you asked me. I was just a rookie pro wrestler back then, waiting for my bout later in the evening, but man, you guys inspired me. I pulverized that girl that night. It was how I got my first agent and signed my first endorsement deal. You helped launch my pro wrestling career."

"Wow. I'm glad we were able to do that for you. Sounds like quite the story. Why'd you become a state trooper?"

"Eh," she said, "I retired from the circuit. The money was pretty decent, but I got tired of the road, you know?"

Yeah, I knew. It was partly for the same reasons I ended up in Twin Strikes.

"So how'd you end up in Madaga?" I asked.

"Oh, I grew up here. Back when the town was a lot smaller, and the reservation was a nothing but forest and a couple of Quonset hut bingo halls. When the time came for me to hang up my wrestling spurs, I decided to come back to New York State and go into law enforcement. Applied to the State Trooper Academy, made the force, and eventually earned my stripes. Requested I be posted here. This place has changed a lot since then."

"I'll say. So you're in charge here?"

"That's right."

"And you sit out front?"

"At the moment I do. The sheriff from over your way's going to be here soon to talk to your twin brother."

I guess under the circumstances, instead of putting some namby-pamby receptionist out front, she wanted to be the first to see whatever person, prayer, or problem might come slinking in through the front door. Which, at the moment, happened to be me.

"I hope your brother's not in any kind of danger or trouble," she said.

"Me too. Do you know why he's here?"

"No. Not really. Sheriff Lawton called and asked us to escort him here for safekeeping. We let your brother drive his own car over but followed along, keeping a close eye on him. All I know is your sheriff and a deputy are on the way to question him about some kind of an investigation. Lawton says he'll brief me when he gets here. Can I get you guys a sandwich or something?"

"No thanks," I said, wondering what she meant by *safekeeping*. "I could use a bottle of water, if you have any. And I was hoping to talk with Bo."

"I don't see why not." She turned to call over her shoulder. "Hey, Malcolm. Can you rustle up a couple of bottles of water for Mr. Gills here? I'm going to take him back to see his brother."

A fellow trooper with skin that looked like he'd just come in from a long day in the cornfield poked his head out from an adjacent office. "Sure thing, Sergeant."

# 15

I followed Maracle around a corner toward the back of the building, the big gun on her hip swaying as she moved. No way that was a standard issue trooper handgun. Was it meant to Dirty Harry lawbreakers into submission? I hoped I never had to find out.

"Have to admit, I haven't kept up with you and your brother's careers," she said. "Do either of you bowl in tournaments anymore?"

"I do sometimes, but not Bo. His shoe business has gotten too big."

"Mmmm-huh. Must be pulling in some money too. I figured as much from the Range Rover outside."

"You think he's in some kind of danger?"

"Your brother? I hope not. When Sheriff Lawton called, I just thought he was some Partridgeberry big-shot who was a potential material witness or something. I don't like missing things, especially when they're right in front of me. I should've realized right off he was Bo Gills."

"Well, now you know."

"How are things going at your bowling alley these days? I saw on the news you guys had a little trouble a few weeks back." She started chuckling. "You managed to put Twin Strikes on the map for a little while."

"Don't remind me."

She laughed. "Okay. I won't. I keep meaning to take a trip up there to the lake, but you know how it goes. No time."

"We'd love to see you. First responders bowl free at Split City."

"No kidding? You know we've got our own alley here at the casino now."

"So I've heard." I'd also realized we were losing some business to the newer, fancier bowling facility, even though we were more than an hour apart.

"Hey, I just remembered… I've got one of my bowling balls out in the truck. You think I could get you and Bo to sign it before you leave?"

"Be happy to."

We reached the end of a long hallway where a door stood open into an interview room with a table and chairs.

Billy sat in a chair behind the table with his eyes closed and his hands folded on his lap.

"Hey, Bo Gills," Maracle said in a voice that seemed a few decibels too loud for the situation. "You might want to wake up. You've got company."

Billy startled, his chair shifting as his eyes flew open wide.

"Wha—? Sorry," he said. "I must've dozed off."

"Not a problem," Maracle said. "Happens a lot around here. Why didn't you tell us you were Bo Gills, the former pro bowler? All your sheriff said was that you were a business owner with no criminal record, so I didn't bother investigating further. Figured I'd wait for him."

Bo looked at the big state trooper, confused. "I don't know. I guess I didn't think the bowling mattered."

"Didn't matter. Are you kidding me? As I was explaining to your brother, Billy, here, I'm a fan. Even have a pair of original TreadBos sitting in my closet next to my bowling bag. To have the two of you here in my office at the same time...well, knock me down with a feather."

"Thank you," Bo mumbled.

He glanced at me. I shrugged.

"I don't know exactly what's going on here," the big woman with the badge said. "Sheriff Lawton said something about an investigation. I hope when he arrives, we can get this all straightened out for you."

"Yeah. I hope we can get it figured out, too." I was tempted to interject some more information about the lookalike and the dead body and everything but decided I'd better wait. I wasn't even supposed to be here. Besides, I needed to speak with Bo before the sheriff got here.

There was a soft knock at the door. It was the other trooper with our bottles of water.

Maracle rose to leave. "Well, I'll leave you two brothers to talk until Lawton arrives. You let us know if you need anything in the meantime. Oh, and one more thing, Billy. You need to give me your cell phone. It's policy. No exceptions."

"Sure. No problem," I said, pulling my phone from my jacket pocket and handing it over.

"Thanks. We'll keep your phone, along with Bo's here, secure until you're done. And don't forget you promised to sign that ball for me before the two of you go."

# 16

"Wow. Isn't she a piece of work?" Bo said after she left.

"Yeah," I said. "I kind of like her."

"Because she's a fan?"

"Call it a gut feeling."

He looked exhausted. And scared.

Bo wore his hair longer than mine and was more fastidious about grooming his carefully styled cut. He owned dozens of pairs of bowling shoes and wore them as a fashion statement, as he was now, along with his dark jeans and some sort of colorful European style soccer jersey. Women were sometimes drawn to him—maybe because of his money. His tasteful Swiss watch no doubt cost more than my 4Runner. But here, in this place, none of that seemed to matter.

"Thanks for coming," he said.

"Of course," I said. "What have you been told?"

"Nothing. The state troopers just said they wanted to bring me over me over here for questioning, and that Sheriff Lawton was on his way from Partridgeberry.

I don't know why they had to serve a warrant and search the factory, let alone bring me here."

"Maybe they just want to make sure you're okay. Did anybody tell you they identified the guy they found near your office?"

"No. What going on?"

I filled him in on what Sheriff Lawton had told me about Bouchard. He interrupted me before I could finish. Clearly, he was nervous.

"I never heard of this guy Bouchard. What does any of this have to do with me?"

"I don't know. But I got a bad feeling after talking to Lawton. Which is why I drove over here."

"Do you trust him?"

"The sheriff? Yes. At least as far as I know him."

"I haven't received any threats. I haven't done anything illegal that I know of. And I checked again with my bank this morning. Everything seems fine. You know I'm supposed to be on a panel speaking to five hundred people later this afternoon, right?"

"Yeah, you told me."

I heard the sound of Sheriff Lawton's voice down the hall.

"Looks like the sheriff is finally here," Bo said.

There was a perfunctory knock on the door before it opened. The sheriff entered, followed by investigator Scriblow. Neither one looked pleased.

"Billy," the sheriff began, "I get that you felt like you had to come, but we're going to have to ask you to leave now. We need to talk to your brother alone."

They glared at me.

What could I do? I desperately wanted to know what was going on, but I had no power here. I did as he asked and left the room.

The trooper who'd brought me the water was waiting for me outside the door to walk me back up to the front of the building. No VIP escort me this time. Trooper Maracle was nowhere in sight.

"Where's the Sergeant?" I asked.

"I'm not sure." The trooper shrugged. "Here you go." He handed me my phone. "But she said you can wait for your brother, if you want."

"All right. I'll be right back."

I went outside and checked on Herk in the dunge. He seemed to be doing fine. Then I walked back in and took a seat in a small waiting area.

#

I spent the next forty-five minutes trying to distract myself with a back issue of *Field & Stream*. I learned five different ways to tie a fishing fly. I learned how to better stalk a deer and a way to make a solar lantern using nothing but tinfoil and duct tape. None of these served to take my mind off what might be happening in the back interview room.

Why were they taking so long?

A door opened from in back, and Sergeant Maracle finally appeared. But something had clearly changed. She didn't look at me; she acted as if I didn't exist. A pit the size of a grapefruit formed in my stomach as she turned away.

The next thing I knew, I spotted Sheriff Lawton and Deputy Scriblow walking down the hallway with Bo. Lawton and Scriblow were on either side of my brother, each with a hand on Bo, who was in handcuffs with his wrists held out in front of him.

For a moment, I was too stunned to speak.

"What the heck is going on here?" I finally managed to splutter.

The sheriff shot me a clinical look. "Your brother is under arrest. He's been read his rights and knows he's entitled to legal counsel. You'll be able to visit him tomorrow at the jail in Partridgeberry before his arraignment."

"Under arrest?" For a moment, I felt the room spin like the rotation of a bowling ball about to strike the pocket. I tried to catch Bo's attention, but his head was down, his eyes locked on the floor. "This has got be a mistake."

"Let it go," the sheriff said. "We don't want to have to charge you with obstruction."

"But he—" I started to yell but quickly lowered my voice, figuring I better cool it for now. "What about Bo's car and all of his stuff at his hotel?"

"The Range Rover is being impounded. We'll be searching his hotel room as well. And all of his personal and company belongings, including his cell phone and computer, are being logged in as potential evidence."

They continued on toward the door. From the look on his face, I could see the sheriff took no pleasure in arresting someone he knew, but he also seemed determined to do his job.

"Can you at least tell me what he's being charged with?" I asked. I felt helpless, like someone was taking a chainsaw to a part of who I was.

It was Scriblow who delivered the news.

"The murder of Etienne Bouchard," he said.

"Are you kidding me?" I had to stop myself from slapping my face to make sure I wasn't dreaming.

I glanced at Sergeant Maracle in her state trooper uniform. She was back sitting behind the counter, not making eye contact with me. Her face had turned ashen, and her lips were pursed as if she'd eaten something disagreeable.

I guessed the bowling ball autograph session would have to wait.

# 17

Our father, Wilson Gills, owned a tiny private air charter service called Upstate Air. Other than his part-time mechanic Len, Dad, as pilot, was the sole employee. Dad flew a Beechcraft Baron and mostly made his living ferrying General Electric or IBM executives out of Albany or Binghamton on short hops around the Northeastern US with occasional forays down south or up into Canada.

My mother's name was Gertrude Gills. Having married into the initials G.G., she grew to be proud of the designation and sometimes had it stenciled onto things she owned like handbags or dishtowels, even a couple of sweaters. All the time I knew her she would sign her letters and postcards, end eventually her emails with that designation. G.G. became a nickname for her as well, among a small cohort of friends and relatives.

My parents took us to church every Sunday. That being said, I wouldn't exactly call them devout. They were religious about one thing, however: bowling.

Every Sunday afternoon, snow or sleet or rain or shine, they would cart Bo and me to what was then a thriving sixteen-lane bowling alley on the outskirts of our little town. We would play all afternoon, sometimes four, five, or six games at once. Bo and I got to be pretty good for our age. We competed with one another like baby-faced gladiators. We fussed and argued about scores, even coming to tears now and then.

Mom was usually embarrassed by our saber-toothed determination to outdo one another. "Now boys," she would say. "You need to calm yourselves down. You know we love you two the same."

But Dad thought our competitive rivalry was great. "Iron sharpens irons, boys. Keep at it. Winners never quit. The harder you work, the luckier you will get."

*Winners never quit.*

All of those old cliches he used to spout—I remembered riding his philosophy for years, and letting it define my life. I remembered having that little saying taped on my bathroom mirror all the time I was traveling on the pro tour.

The sad thing was our parents died within a month of one another. Bo and I were in our twenties back then and still on tour. I was walking into an alley in Pocatello, Idaho, for the second day in a weekend tournament that I was leading when I got the call about Dad.

He'd been flying two passengers back from a weekend trip to Montreal when the heart attack came on. The two passengers, a man and a woman, later testified it didn't happen all at once—not like some heart attack stories you hear. But Dad had somehow managed to bring the plane into Massena for a safe landing. Both passengers spoke about how he'd refused their help—not that they could have done much, though one had been trained as a nurse—but focused instead on his job of bringing them down safely. He died before the EMTs could get him to a hospital. The passengers said he was hero.

Mom's death was less of a surprise. She'd been suffering with breast cancer for a few years and had gone through three or four rounds of chemotherapy. G.G. had always been a fighter, but after Dad died, it was as if she'd lost the will to live and decided it was her time to go as well. She was only fifty-five, and while Dad was much older, he'd never seemed that old.

Every now and then, when I was working the late shift alone at Split City and had locked the doors for the night, I would go to my office and pull a cold beer from the fridge. I'd sit down in my comfortable chair, prop my feet up on my old desk, and look across the room at a glass case in the middle of the floor on the opposite wall.

Inside stood a pair of bowling balls on stands, two bags, and two pairs of shoes. I could still see the honored place those bags, with the balls and shoes inside, held in the closet of our little makeshift half-Victorian, half-ranch house back home. A red one for Mom. Black for Dad. I could still hear the crash of the pins from watching one of them throw a strike in the pocket when I was a little boy. I could still smell the faint scent of dried lane oil left in the bags, the sweet aroma of tomato sauce from Mom cooking something Italian in the kitchen, even though she wasn't Italian, whenever I got back home.

#

In a daze, I trudged outside, watching as the sheriff and his deputy loaded Bo in handcuffs into the sheriff's cruiser, where I'd sat myself not too long before. What now?

After they drove off, I crossed the parking lot to where Herk was still waiting for me in the front seat of the dunge. His big tail wagged at the sight of me.

I climbed in and slammed the door. "Sorry to have to leave you out here alone for so long, buddy."

The big dog poked his nose across the seat and licked my ear.

I sat petting Herk and tried to make some sense of what had just happened. Why was Bo being charged with murder and why so soon after they'd found the body? If he was over here in Madaga, how could he have murdered Bouchard, and how could Bouchard's body have ended up in Partridgeberry? Clearly the sheriff knew more than he'd been telling me. But if Bo was innocent—and I had to believe he was—why would they be arresting him?

I started the engine and let the feeble heater begin to warm the cab as best it could. Before too long, a tow truck appeared. The driver began hooking up Bo's Range Rover to haul it away. I plugged in my cell phone as I watched.

"What do you think, pal? Should we just head back home and wait until I can go see Bo tomorrow?"

He looked at me, wagging his tail.

"You're right," I said. "We need to figure out what's really going on. Let's just hope I don't end up in jail like him."

I fastened my seat belt, preparing to back up and pull out of the lot.

As if in response to my decision, my phone began to ring. The display told me it was Carianne, Bo's assistant from TreadBo. Had she already heard the news?

I took a deep breath and answered.

"Billy," she said. "Thank God. Where's Bo? The sheriff was here and people from his office, and they took lots of files. I sent him a message via someone at the convention and have been trying to reach him for the past couple of hours about his files and other things they took from the factory."

"I know. I tried to come by the factory earlier, but they wouldn't let me in. Bo knows they were there too."

"Do you know where Bo is?"

"Yes," I said. "I'm over here in Madaga and just spent some time with him."

"Oh, wow. Well, can you tell him I need to talk to him too right away?" She sounded anxious.

"Umm…that might not be possible for a while."

"Why? What's going on?"

"Bo's been arrested for murder."

There was a long pause.

"He what?" she asked.

"There was a body found in Partridgeberry yesterday morning. Bo's been arrested and is being charged with killing the man."

"Billy, if this is some kind of a sick joke…"

"It's no joke. I'm sitting here in the parking lot outside the state police barracks in Madaga. They just took Bo into custody. Taking him to jail in Partridgeberry. I watched them walk him out in handcuffs and tow away his Range Rover."

There was another, even longer silence on the line. I thought I heard sniffling.

"Are you okay?" I asked.

For quite a while, I'd suspected Carianne of having feelings for Bo. I couldn't point to anything specific—just the way I'd observed her interacting with him and how she looked at him sometimes. I even asked Bo about it once, but he brushed the idea away. All he ever talked about when it came to his assistant was how smart she was and how glad he was that he'd hired her.

"I'll be all right," she said. "Is Bo okay?"

"He seemed to be as stunned as I was. They said I won't be able to talk to him again until tomorrow before his arraignment."

"What about a lawyer?"

"I don't know who he would hire for something like this. The only legal work we've been involved with together has to do with business and contracts. Nothing criminal."

"Maybe your old girlfriend can recommend someone. Isn't she a lawyer?"

"Yes, but I wouldn't count on her for anything," I said. The last person I wanted to talk to right now was Justine.

"This is just unbelievable. Everything seems to be going crazy all of a sudden."

"What do you mean?"

"Well, first, there was that disaster at the conference in Twin Strikes last month. Then today, like I told you, the sheriff shows up here in the factory with a warrant, and all of the deputies searching the offices. The production guys even stopped working for the morning. Then Max Fontainebleau shows up."

"Fontainebleau was there too?" I asked. "After the sheriff?"

"Yes. And he starts breathing down my neck in his creepy way, telling me he needs to talk with Bo right away and that's it's urgent. Said he'd been leaving messages for Bo, but no answer. Seemed like he was about ready to blow a gasket. Now you call and tell me this. I figured something really bad had to be going on. I'm scared for Bo."

"Yeah, me too. But don't worry. It has to be some kind of huge screwup." At least I hoped it was. "We'll get it figured out. Did Fontainebleau say anything else?"

"I don't know. He was ranting and raving about a huge amount of money, some kind of investment, and he mentioned Giuseppe Rhodes."

"Rhodes? The guy from Pontefio?"

"Yeah. Because they distribute some of our shoes, he was here last year touring the factory. Fontainebleau was here then too."

"All right," I said. "Here's what I'd like you do. Call Fontainebleau and tell him I want to meet with him this evening, as soon as I get back from Madaga. I imagine he already knows by now, or will soon, about Bo being arrested."

"What time do you think you'll be back?"

"Give me until seven. I've got something important I need to check into first."

"Okay, I'll text you to confirm."

"Thanks. And let's try to keep this quiet for the time being. Word's bound to leak out sooner rather than later, but we don't want people leaving in a panic from the factory."

"A couple of them have left already. I'm getting a lot of questions. Everybody's wondering what's going on."

"Just do the best you can."

"All right," she said. "I'll try."

"Thanks again. You're the best," I said. "I don't know what Bo would do without you."

I could almost imagine her blushing before we hung up. I put the car in gear and pulled out of the lot, turning to head back into Madaga.

# 18

The Great Madaga Casino, Hotel, and Convention Center featured a multistory parking garage. For high rollers, there was valet parking with attendants attired in shirts and jackets tastefully styled in Native American themes. Not being a high roller, I parked on the fourth level.

I didn't like the idea of leaving Herk alone in a public garage, so I rummaged around in my trunk and found my homemade service dog vest. It wasn't right. But I'd only used it once before, and this was an emergency.

I needed to find Rhodes. From what Bo had told me, Giuseppe Rhodes would have been one of the last people to see him the night of the murder.

Herk and I crossed the skybridge from the garage to the casino. He seemed elated to finally get out to stretch his legs. And who knew what great smells or canine adventures awaited in the bright lights and bowels of the Great Madaga?

We approached the main entrance where a pair of security guards, one of them waving a wand metal detector, stood waiting to give us a thorough inspection.

"Here for some gaming, sir?" the one with the detector asked as we approached.

"Absolutely."

"Welcome," he said stepping up to us. "Would you mind lifting your arms and opening your jacket for a moment so I can scan you? My partner here can hold your animal. I assume the dog's trained."

"Of course."

Herk was trained all right. Of course, that depended how you defined trained.

All was going well until Herk spotted a wire hanging from the second guard's taser. The taser was attached to the man's belt, and, well, what can I say, Herk has a thing for loose wires. When he finally let go of the thing, in the uncomfortable silence and smiles that followed, the second guard managed to blurt out something to the effect of, "Have a nice day, sir."

Down the corridor, I scratched the retriever's ear and whispered, "Hey, buddy, you've got to behave a little better than that or you're going to get us both kicked out of here."

Herk wagged his tail and panted.

Off to an auspicious start, I tried to look at least somewhat interested in the first row of slot machines as we passed. They came in all shapes and sizes.

Chrome and electronics. Long handles with bulbous heads. An elderly couple sat beside one another playing on different units, the man decked out in a white checkerboard sport coat, the woman puffing away on a cigarette. You could tell they were a couple because each time they played a roll, they'd reached out to clasp one another's hand for moral support. I hoped to God they weren't gambling away their Social Security money.

Herk gave a tug on the leash, his curiosity piqued, perhaps by a familiar noise emanating from a huge space adjacent to one corner of the casino. It was the sound of a bowling ball striking the pins.

*Great.*

We'd been hearing from Split City customers about our much bigger competitor's expected opening for months. Now here it was in all its glory: The Great Madaga Family Bowling and Entertainment Center. As if I didn't have enough problems with my twin brother being carted off to jail.

How "family" went along with the crushed cigarettes and hard drinks of the casino was beyond me. The dividing line between the casino and the alley was a fashionable brick-and-stone frontage with a commercial Tuscan feel. Before I could even get to the forty-eight bowling lanes, I had to pass by a house-sized check-in area, which featured, among other things, the bright neon lights of a something called a "Fun

Palace and Childcare Center." Past that mini-complex, I came upon a state-of-the art two-story video game arcade that featured everything from *Pac Man* to *Halo* war games to Indy and NASCAR-style racing consoles. If that wasn't enough, there was an actual rock-climbing wall complete with a waiting teenage attendant. Next came a towering ceiling-to-floor waterfall that had been built around an eighteen-hole indoor miniature golf course. And on the far end, safely positioned away from the kids, stood the coup de grace: a full-service restaurant, bar, and craft beer outlet that included multiple billiards and ping-pong tables, darts, and foosball. According to a sign on the wall, Great Madaga had even commissioned a regional craft brewer to supply them with their own in-house beer, an IPA said to have a distinctive blend of apple and oak notes with hints of citrus.

Even worse, the place was busy for a weekday lunch hour. The bowling lanes were more than half full, people of all ages. Even some actual families. What, didn't kids still have to go to school? My heart sank.

"We should've stuck to the casino," I said to Herk.

But I even seemed to have lost my wing dog, who was eyeing the adjacent pet care center, where five or six pooches of all shapes and sizes were roaming around and playing together on a fake grass field sprinkled liberally with indoor pet relief stations.

"Turncoat," I said. "Maybe instead of Hercules we should have named you Benedict Arnold."

Herk gave a little whimper as we turned to go.

"You know what though, buddy? Let's face it. You and I own a charming little dive of any alley. But compared to this place, we're a slowly dying throwback to a day gone by."

He panted away, ignoring me.

"You're right," I said. "At the moment, we have a bigger mission."

Turning back toward the casino, I spotted what I was looking for: an entranceway along the gaming floor that led to the adjacent Great Madaga Hotel. Soon enough, we'd made our way to the outer hotel lobby, where a tasteful bank of house telephones hung in booths with comfortable seats made of real hand-carved wood.

But before I could move toward the phone, I felt a buzzing from my jacket pocket and sighed as I pulled out my phone.

Justine was calling. Just the person I did not want to talk to. I considered ignoring the call but knew she'd keep pestering me.

"Hey," I said, answering. "What's up?"

"Hey to you, too. I called the alley to see how you and Herk were doing since you always take him to work with you, but Petula said you hadn't come in today. Is something wrong? Where are you?"

The last thing I needed right now was my ex still stalking me from a thousand miles away.

"Everything's fine. I'm at the casino over in Madaga."

"What? The casino?" she said. "Is Herk with you?"

"Right here by my side. Happy as a pooch can be."

"He better be. You don't gamble. What are you doing at a casino?"

"I had some business to attend to. It's complicated."

"Complicated, huh. I'll bet. My guess is it involves another woman."

Justine thought everything in my life should have revolved around her, which was part of her problem.

"Well, it's not that. And I don't have time to get into it with you right now. Herk's doing just fine."

"How'd you get them to let you bring him into the casino?"

"It was no problem," I lied.

"You didn't use that stupid service dog vest you made, did you? Like the time that woman kicked you out of the farmer's market in Partridgeberry?"

"Yeah, she was a crowd Nazi all right. But no one's giving us any trouble here. Listen, Herk and I have got to go. There's somebody here we need to talk to. Go and have fun at your conference."

I hung up before she could respond.

# 19

Herk and I approached the house phones. I'd barely put the handset up to my ear when a perky sounding voice answered the call.

"It's a great day at the Great Madaga. How may I help?"

*You could help improve my day,* I thought, *because it's looking pretty terrible.* "Ah, sure, could you connect me with one of your guests? The name is Giuseppe Rhodes."

"Absolutely. Mr. Rhodes. He's in one of our top floor suites. Connecting you now, sir."

I thanked her and waited. The phone rang several times, and I was just about to hang up, when a weary sounding voice answered.

It was a woman.

"I'm looking for Mr. Rhodes."

"He's not here at the moment," she said. "He's down at the booth, I think. Supposed to give a speech later or something."

"This is Billy Gills. Bo Gills's brother."

"Gills. Oh, yeah, the TreadBo guy. Hi. My name's Erica Glanders. I work for Pontefio, and I'm up here running tech support. You here for the panel? I think Bo and Giuseppe are both talking this afternoon."

"Yeah. Well, it turns out Bo's not going to be able to make it this afternoon."

"Really? Okay, why don't I text Mr. Rhodes. I'll tell him you're here."

"That would be great."

I waited on the line. A few seconds later, she said, "Here we go. He says to meet him at the booth. You can't miss it. Pontefio's got a huge space just inside the convention entrance."

"All right, thanks," I said. "I'm heading there now."

There are some advantages to being an identical twin. When I went to bluff my way on to the convention floor without a badge, I was stopped by a heavy-set security guard, who must have made me as a gate crasher. But he was instantly overruled by his supervisor, a man with a walkie talkie, who was talking with some convention officials a few feet away. He glanced at me and called out, "It's okay, James. He's one of the exhibitors."

I nodded a thanks. James stepped aside and Herk and I moved on.

Inside, the convention floor was an explosion of color and shoes and light. It spread out over an open area the size of three or four football fields. Pontefio was a publicly traded company that dwarfed TreadBo in size, and Pontefio's world of shoes booth was the size of a small house. It smelled pleasantly of leather and hummed with the quiet resonance of people admiring the latest creations, all of which were a part of or endorsed by the Pontefio brand. You could scarcely avoid passing through the display on your way into the convention floor.

"Billy!"

I heard Giuseppe Rhodes before I saw him. At least, from what Bo had told me about him, I assumed it might be Rhodes. It was hard to miss his aristocratic tone.

"It is you, right? Bo has told me all about you, and you're not dressed like him."

I said nothing. Come to think of it, I guess my jeans and hiking boots did look a little out of place in the casino and on the convention floor. No wonder the security guard at the entrance had pegged me as an interloper.

"What's this I hear about Bo not being able to make our panel?" he asked. "Is he ill or something?"

"We need to talk," I said.

"Of course." He glanced at the big expensive-looking chronograph adorning his well-tanned wrist. "I've got ninety minutes before the panel is scheduled to begin. Why don't you let me get you something to eat or drink?"

He turned and led me toward the nearest wall of the convention hall. "We've got a private meeting room reserved just off floor," he explained.

Rhodes's charismatic smile projected a commanding presence. A middle-aged stocky figure with a shock of white hair and a perfectly trimmed, equally white mustache, his eyes seemed to take in everything, sifting, analyzing.

Even as he listened, he would cross his arms or lean forward in an aggressive posture, demanding the speaker pay attention to his presence. When he spoke, he amplified his words by gesturing at the air with his hands. I figured his aura of Italian sophistication, whether genuine or not, must have been an advantage for him in the shoe business. For most people, whether they be middle-aged women or teens in the inner city, shoes made some sort of a fashion statement.

"I see you're wearing TreadBo hiking boots," he said as we walked. "Although, I must say, they look a bit worn."

"Shows they can take the mileage," I shot back.

"Uh-huh." He didn't look convinced.

"Well, I like them. They're comfortable," I said, caught off guard by the snub.

"Of course," he said, diplomatically. "I suppose that's what really matters in the end."

Rhodes sported a pair of supple black loafers that probably cost several times my monthly mortgage payment. He glanced down at Herk, who was behaving for the moment, trotting along on the leash beside me. "And who's your friend here?" he asked.

"His name's Hercules."

"Hercules is a good name." He didn't elaborate or ask me why I'd brought the dog into the building with a service vest. Probably just as well.

I followed him toward one of the walls of the cavernous space. There, a carpeted corridor formed by dark cords held up by guidance stanchions led to an automatic sliding glass door. A guard standing at the end of the carpet nodded to Rhodes and stepped by to let us past. I suddenly felt like a VIP.

Inside the glass door, we came to a hallway lined with private rooms. Rhodes held an access key card to a sensing plate that unlocked the door to the first room on the right.

"What can I get you to drink?" he asked, opening the door for me. "We've got all sorts of juices, soft drinks, sparkling waters. None of the stronger stuff, I'm afraid. That's upstairs."

"Nothing for me, thanks."

I took a seat inside. Herk lay down at my feet, and I waited until Rhodes closed the door behind him.

"Bo's been arrested," I said.

"You must be joking," he said.

He seemed prepared to discount the revelation. But one look at my face, and his confident demeanor melted away. He shook his head as if he were trying to recover from a hard punch to the face.

"I'm not kidding," I said. "He was escorted by state police to their barracks here in Madaga, and the Partridgeberry County Sheriff came over here and took him into custody. They're transporting him to jail as we speak."

"Jail? Whatever for?"

"All I know is, he's under arrest."

It wasn't the whole truth, of course. But I didn't want to tell him too much. Something about him made me wary.

"I don't understand," he said.

"I'm still trying to figure it all out myself."

"You know someone from your sheriff's office contacted me earlier this morning. A Deputy Scriblow. Now it makes sense."

"What did Scriblow want?"

"He asked if I was with Bo the night before last. I told him that I was, and I told him about our party. He wanted to know exactly what time Bo left. I told him I couldn't say exactly but gave him my best guess. Which was around nine o'clock. I asked him if Bo was all right. He assured me he was fine. I texted Bo, but he didn't respond, so I assumed maybe he'd had his laptop stolen or something."

I knew enough to understand that the police didn't have to divulge complete information or tell the truth when questioning someone. It looked like they were playing that game with Rhodes. Maybe me, too.

"I'm just trying to figure out what really happened," I said. "Is there anything else you can tell me?"

"Well, it might not even need mentioning. But I'm sure you know that TreadBo and your brother have been under some financial pressure recently. Especially after that event of yours last month. It doesn't help that there's been a downturn in the shoe market of late."

This was something of a surprise. Outside of the alley, Bo never talked to me much about either his personal or his company's finances, and certainly not about how the shoe market was doing. Unlike his twin brother, he always seemed to be thriving personally, with plenty of money to spare.

"Anyway," Rhodes babbled on, "I'm sure TreadBo's just going through a rough patch. These kinds of things happen all the time in our business. I don't like the sounds of him getting arrested though. Bo's a good soul, and I'd hate to see him getting mixed up in anything bad. His company needs him. I have some other friends in the business running smaller to midsize companies like Bo. Good people. But in the end, it all comes down to them. It's not like they have all of the resources a larger company like we at Pontefio have. Your brother is a creative, free spirit. Our business needs people like him."

This guy sure knew how to turn on the charm. No wonder he was a CEO. He reminded me of some of the politicians I'd met.

"What are you going to tell people here at the convention about his arrest?" I asked.

"Nothing really. Not yet. I can cover for Bo and make excuses for him this afternoon on the panel. Although I'm afraid the news is bound to leak out soon enough."

"All right. Anything else you can tell me?"

"No, I don't believe so. Is there anything else I can do to help?"

"I don't think so. Not right now." I took Herk by the leash and rose from the table. "I'm sorry, but I have to go."

I needed to get back to the factory in Partridgeberry to see if anyone was there I could talk to.

"Of course. You go and see about your brother," he said.

# 20

It was after dark by the time Herk and I made it to the TreadBo factory in Partridgeberry. Only a couple of cars remained in the lot.

Light filled the lobby, but the rest of the building was dark, except for some of the offices upstairs. I clipped Herk to his leash and we walked in the front door. Ralph was seated at his usual spot but with a glum look on his face.

"Sad day, Billy," he said.

"Tell me about it. I guess you've heard."

"Everybody's heard," he said. "I'm so sorry."

"Thanks. Who's left in the building?"

"Carianne's still up there, and so is Zune."

"Okay. Can I take the elevator?"

"I've shut it down for the night, but you can take the stairs. Stairwell door's open."

"All right. Thanks."

"If you see Bo, tell him we're all thinking about him. Whatever's going on, I don't see any way he could have been mixed up in it, let alone killed somebody."

"Me either," I said before Herk and I headed into the stairs.

#

A young man appeared down the hall as we emerged from the stairwell on the second floor. Tan T-shirt, black jeans, dark-rimmed glasses. He was holding a notebook computer and staring at the screen as he walked. He looked up and caught sight of me.

"Billy," he said. "What the heck is going on?" Mark Zune, the company's head of data processing, had been part of TreadBo since the early days. He was one of the few people who'd actually learned to tell Bo and me apart on sight.

"I was hoping you could tell me," I said as we came together.

"There's all sorts of rumors flying around. The sheriff and some deputies swooped in here like the Gestapo this morning and took a bunch of stuff. Somebody just called Carianne and said Bo's in jail. Is it true? Has there been an accident or something? And why do you have your dog with you?"

Zune's mind worked like a kinetic sponge. I was used to his rapid-fire questions. He always seemed to have five things going at the same time.

"Yes, it's true Bo's in jail," I said. "We need to talk. Is Carianne still here?"

"Yeah. She's in her office. We're the only ones still here."

"Let's go. I'll fill you both in."

He folded his laptop, and I followed him down the hallway to Carianne's office, weighing how much to tell them. Until I could talk to Bo at the jail in the morning, I needed to be careful. Assuming my twin wasn't lying to me or guilty of killing someone, that is.

We found Carianne sitting in her office, working on some financial reports on her computer.

"Billy!" She leaped out of her chair to greet me. "I can't believe this is happening. She repeated the same kind of questions Zune had asked. "And you have your dog with you. Oh, my gosh." She bent down to pet Herk, who panted his appreciation.

"Let's sit down, and I'll bring you up to speed as best I can," I said.

She took a seat back at the desk in front of the computer while Zune and I sat in a couple of side chairs. Herk, content to be around people, lay down on the floor.

I gave them a quick, superficial rundown about how Bo had been arrested and accused of a serious crime. I didn't go into any detail, especially about the body I'd been asked to identify—just gave the basic information because, really, that's about all I still knew myself.

"Wow." Zune ran his fingers through his hair when I was through. "This is completely insane."

"Never in a million years could I have imagined something like this," Carianne said. "Are you sure Bo's all right?"

"I hope so. Knowing Bo, he would have lined up a lawyer by now. They're probably looking at the evidence the police have against him. The sheriff's office won't let me go see him until tomorrow morning. But maybe I'll be able to talk to the lawyer."

"Who is that?" she asked.

"I'm not sure. I was hoping you might be able to give me a clue."

"Well, we have a corporate attorney from the city, but I don't know anything about a lawyer to help him or the company to deal with something like this."

"Okay," I said. "I'll see what I can do to find out. Unless they contact me first."

Then I suddenly remembered Petula up at Split City. She was probably dying with curiosity—wondering why I'd been acting so strange.

I glanced at my phone. "I'm gonna have to go in a minute, but I do have a couple of questions for you both."

"Of course," said Carianne.

"Anything," said Zune.

"You told me Bo was by himself at the convention because your marketing director, Addison Foley, felt ill."

"Yes," Carianne said. "I've been talking to Addison on the phone. He was running a fever over the weekend, but he's better today."

"Okay," I said. *One more person I need to talk to.*

"I was supposed to go in Addison's place," Zune offered, "but had to back out at the last minute because we've been having a big problem with our main server, and it's been causing issues with a couple of our automated machines. So Bo stepped in, and I think they were able to add him at the last minute to speak on a panel."

"You say you've been having a big server problem," I said. "Any chance you may have been hacked?" I remembered what the sheriff had said about the Etienne Bouchard's criminal history and computer skills.

He shrugged. "I suppose. Anything's possible at this point. I'm still trying to unpack it."

He launched into some technical explanation about programming code. Zune loved to talk tech and assumed everyone else spoke the language. But right now, I had bigger things on my mind.

I held up my hand for him to stop. "It's okay, Mark. I get it."

"Oh." Carianne shook her head and looked like she was about to cry. "I still can't believe this is happening.

And right when the factory's beginning to struggle with money."

"Is that because of what happened at the conference last month?" I asked.

"Partly. Yes." She turned back toward her computer to glance at a financial spreadsheet on her screen. As she did, I noticed a plastic milk container with its top cut off, like the kind people use to collect raffle tickets, tucked behind her plant in the corner, but I paid it no mind.

"Can you tell me more about the company finances?"

"Well. Even before the conference, things weren't great. Bo's probably told you about our profits being down."

Actually, he hadn't, at least not until lately. But I let her go on.

She wrinkled her nose and pressed her lips together. "If things don't begin to improve soon, the fear around here is that the company may have to begin making some layoffs."

"Did Bo tell you that?"

"Well, no. Not in so many words."

"But he does talk to you about a lot of things to do with the company."

"Of course."

"Bo's always singing your praises. He tells me you're super organized and efficient."

She smiled. "Yes. I try. And I also believe in Bo and our company brand." She proudly lifted the leg of her jeans to show her TreadBo boots.

Ralph appeared in the doorway to Carianne's office. Still the glum look on his face. "Hey, folks," he said. "Sorry to interrupt but I'm clocking out."

"That's all right, Ralph," she said. "We'll lock up before we leave."

"Okay, you got it." He told everybody good night and disappeared back down the hall.

"All right," I said. "Anything else I need to know right now before I go too?" I was still thinking of Petula at the alley and how I needed to break the news to her. That is, if she hadn't heard already.

"Yes," she replied. "Remember what I told you about Max Fontainebleau? Well, he's been sniffing around here even more the past couple of days. He came by yesterday, and I heard he was chatting up a few people in the factory."

"Yeah," Zune chimed in. "That guy gives me the creeps. With his big resort and all. He may be one of our county supervisors, but I never voted for him."

"Did either of you see him talking to anybody else?" I asked.

"Yes," Carianne said, wrinkling up her nose. "Before the sheriff and his deputies left, Fontainebleau showed up, like I said. I saw him through the window talking to them for a while out in the parking lot. Then he came up here and was asking me about the company, how the factory was doing and all." She paused. "Awkward. I thought it was weird."

# 21

Back in Twin Strikes, I dropped Herk off with Petula at Split City.

"All right, spill it. What the heck's been going on?" she said. The alley was moderately busy, with four or five lanes in use.

"I'll explain it all in a little bit," I said. "I've got to go see Max Fontainebleau first."

"Fontainebleau? I'm smelling a rat. You know there's a new rumor going around town about he used to be affiliated with the mob."

"Yeah, I've heard that too. But you know how people like to talk. I shouldn't be gone long. Could you make sure Herk gets some dinner while he's here?"

"You bet. We've got a bag of dog food in the kitchen. Be careful, Billy. Speaking of rumors, my friend Melise from over in Partridgeberry called. She said there's word going around about your brother. Something about a dead body and the sheriff and his deputies searching the TreadBo factory? Is this true?"

"Some of it, yes. Like I said, I'll explain it to you when I return."

"Well, all I know is if Fontainebleau's got anything to do with this, you better be watching your back," she said. "I'm going to pray."

#

My headlights cut a swath along the dark highway that wound around the lake on the way to Max Fontainebleau's estate. Fontainebleau lived in a palatial log and stone edifice rumored to have belonged, at one time, to a distant Rockefeller relative. It occupied prime acreage on the most scenic side of Lake Conostowakaka, across from the town and the historic resort.

As I rounded the final curve in the darkness, I saw two oversized stone pillars guarding the entrance to Fontainebleau's giant house. The place was lit up like there was a party going on, although I only spotted a couple of expensive cars in the circular driveway.

I was hoping to catch the supervisor by surprise. Instead, I found him standing alone on the brightly lit front porch with a thick cigar protruding from his mouth.

Almost as if he'd been waiting for me.

He took another puff as my muddy truck sullied his pristine, tastefully lit driveway, illuminating the tip of the cigar and filling the surrounding air with smoke, before removing it and breaking into a big smile.

I brought the dunge to a stop beside the front steps and climbed out.

"Billy! Interesting, isn't it? I was just standing here wondering if you might show up," he said. "Heard about your brother being arrested." His deep, gravelly voice boomed down from the porch like a monarch deigning to address a lowly subject.

He stood a shade over six feet tall and must have weighed close to three hundred pounds. The thick gold watch on his wrist looked expensive, and his black curly hair appeared to have been recently styled. Decades before, Fontainebleau had worked as a club bouncer in Queens, a part of his past he always seemed at pains to remind people about.

I climbed the front porch steps. Shaking his hand felt like touching the meaty paw of a bear.

"It's good to see you…despite the difficult circumstances," he said. Ever the wheeler-dealer and minor politician. "Sorry about your brother."

*Yeah, I'll bet you are.*

Fontainebleau had never before shown much interest in Bo or TreadBo. Other than the fact that he owned the building that housed Split City, I had as little as possible to do with him. Which wasn't always easy.

"I just came from the TreadBo factory," I said. "Seems like you've suddenly taken a keen interest in the goings-on over there."

"Well, you would too you had the kind of dollars I've got invested in that place."

"What do you mean?" I asked. I had no idea what he was talking about.

"Why the money I loaned to the TreadBo factory and to your brother to help them get through their current cash crush of course. Half a mil."

"What are you talking about? He never breathed a word of it to me."

"Ah. So the plot thickens." He smiled.

"What plot?"

"Well, we signed the papers with my lawyer down in the city and transferred the money just last week. Now I find out your brother was somehow working in cahoots with this character he had fixed up to look like himself. Some kind of strange monkey business, you ask me. Maybe he thought he could weasel out of his debt, I don't know. But something must have gone wrong with his plans. Because he ended up offing the guy."

Now I saw why the sheriff had been so circumspect with me about certain things. Whatever they were alleging Bo did, they might have thought I was in on it too, or that I knew about it at least. And with Fontainebleau having so much money on the line, he no doubt had been putting pressure on the sheriff. I couldn't see Sheriff Lawton bowing to political pressure though. He must have had some kind of evidence he thought made sense in order to arrest Bo.

"My brother didn't *off* anybody."

"So you say. But how do you really know for sure? In my experience, people can get pretty crazy and desperate when it comes to money. And, if you don't mind me pointing it out…it's not like your brother hasn't done some stupid things in the past. Take that whole cockamamie Split Down the Middle and bowling for unity thing he orchestrated last month, for example. Your brother and his company have wasted a boatload of cash lately. And you've enabled him."

"Oh, so you're a professional psychologist now too," I said.

Now he was sounding like my ex-girlfriend.

Fontainebleau seemed tired. His face held a drawn expressionless pallor as he took another puff of his cigar. "Suppose you better talk to the authorities about your brother's legal difficulties."

"You're an authority. You're our county supervisor," I said.

"Right. And the creaky Twin Strikes town council is made up of a bunch of backward thinkers I still can't get past."

"You mean because people don't want you securing a casino license."

"You're no politician though, are you, Billy? And last time I looked, you were no detective either."

"Maybe not. But it doesn't take a genius to figure out you probably had something to do with Bo's arrest. You think he stole from you."

"What can I say?" He shrugged again. "I don't like thieves."

"Bo's no thief."

"Yeah, well…we'll see."

"Funny how you just so happened to appear at Split City looking for me the same day the sheriff called me in to identify a body they thought at first was Bo," I said.

I was fishing, but the fact that Bo hadn't said anything to me about the loan made me uncomfortable. That wasn't like Bo. At least, not the Bo I knew. Or was it?

"I wanted to see how the alley's been doing," he said. "I do own the building, you remember. After that stunt of a conference your brother pulled last month, I have to protect my assets. Plus, I've been thinking about making some changes at the resort and wanted to talk to you."

"Now is not a good time for me to talk with you about your resort," I said.

"Gotcha," he said. "Right now, you got bigger fish to fry. Your brother being in jail and all."

Fontainebleau had never consulted me about anything to do with the resort before. Which made me even more suspicious.

"And I don't want to find out you had anything to do with him being there," I said.

He took an exaggerated step back. "What? I'm hurt, Billy. Can't believe you'd ever think such a thing. I'm a businessman. You know that. How's Bo being in jail supposed to help me?"

"I don't know yet."

"Well, I do know. It doesn't help me one bit. You guys with the alley haven't exactly been ideal tenants and all. And now I got this bond in what could suddenly be a shaky company."

"Yeah, you're a real saint, Max. What I'm saying is if you know anything about why this has happened with this Bouchard guy showing up dead and all, I need to hear it."

He looked at me for a long moment. "I can tell you one thing," he said.

I waited.

"You know I don't just throw money at something without doing my due diligence. I did a little research on my own into Bo's company and the industry and all. Some of his distributors and competitors. You get the idea."

I had a hard time envisioning Fontainebleau as a conscientious investor—loan shark was more like it—but I said nothing.

He went on, "I know a guy who's friends with my broker on Wall Street. So I call the guy up and talk to him. He tells me a little bit about the couple of publicly traded companies who are in TreadBo's product space, you know corporate talk—all that sort of rigamarole. Then he tells me about one company in particular, the biggest one, this Pontevecio company, or whatever it's called."

"Pontefio?" I asked.

"Yeah, that's the one. Anyways, guy says there's maybe trouble on the horizon for them. Something about overinflated inventories, not enough new product in the pipeline, that sort of the thing. He says rumors are the board's looking to oust the CEO. I figure it's probably a good time to be investing in TreadBo then, and I give Bo the money. Now the whole thing's gone squirrelly on me."

Could Rhodes have been somehow mixed up in all of this? He'd seemed very sympathetic and helpful at the convention. Maybe a little too helpful. Bo's relationship with Rhodes seemed like an odd relationship, one I'd never completely understood. From what little I knew, Rhodes company was both a competitor for TreadBo's non bowling shoe models, and a distributor for the TreadBo bowling shoes. Seemed like a built-in conflict of interest to me.

"What are you thinking, Billy?" Fontainebleau asked.

"Trying to decide whether or not to believe you. How do I know you're not the one behind framing Bo for murder? You could be angling to try to take control of TreadBo. You just told me yourself, you've got a half million dollars' worth of motive."

He lifted the cigar from his mouth and spat something on the ground. "What do I want with the shoe business and some factory? Too much of a hassle, you ask me. You may not like me, Billy, or the way I do business. But this is not my doing. I've been pretty lenient with the rent a couple of times when you guys went through a real rough patch with Split City too."

"Yeah. Like I said, you're a real saint. I just better not find out you're lying to me."

His face took on a darker expression. "Look, I've been trying to be nice here 'cause you're stressed. But here you are coming to my house, accusing me of something? After I tried to come to your brother's rescue in his time of need? You better think long and hard about that, my friend. Maybe I should be the one accusing you."

"Oh, I'll be thinking, all right. And I'll be back." I turned to get back in the dunge.

"I ain't going nowhere," he said.

#

Carianne had given me her cell phone number before I left the factory. I dialed it from the truck. She answered it after a couple of rings, and I talked to her on the speakerphone as I drove back through the darkness into town.

"Did TreadBo get a large cash infusion from an investor last week?" I asked her.

"What? No. Not to my knowledge. And I take care of the payroll and check the accounts pretty much every day. Not that the factory couldn't probably use an investment like that right now."

"Do you know if Bo has some sort of special private company account?"

"I have no idea what you're talking about," she said. "I'd be surprised if he did. Why? What's going on?"

"Not sure. I'll have to get back to you later," I said. "That's all I need to know for now. Thanks very much."

I stared at the road cutting through the forest along the lake.

Every revelation seemed to bring new questions. Had Fontainebleau really loaned my brother money? Had Bo stolen the money for himself? I thought about Etienne Bouchard, the career criminal who was such a close lookalike for Bo and me. Maybe he'd scammed Fontainebleau out of the money. But how could he have done that without Bo getting wind of it? And would he have gone to such lengths for half a million dollars? Where was the money now, and why was Bouchard dead?

Maybe Fontainebleau found out he'd been duped. Maybe he killed Bouchard or hired someone else to do it. Maybe he was framing Bo for the murder to cover his tracks. I desperately needed to talk to Bo. There had to be more.

Despite it being spring, a few passing snow flurries whispered through the glow of my headlights. Back in town, I sped toward Split City.

# 22

"Bo's in jail," I said.

"Say *what*?" Petula's eyes widened as she sat across from me in my office.

A number of people were still bowling out on the lanes. G was temporarily manning the front desk.

"Why?" she asked.

"He's being charged with murder."

"Murder?" She squinted, looking skeptical. "Stop joking around, Billy."

"I wish I were joking. A lot's been happening that I haven't been able to tell you."

"I'll say." She ran her fingers through her hair and let out a long breath. "Oh, my Lord. How can they charge Bo with murder? Your brother wouldn't hurt a flea."

"Yeah, well tell that to the sheriff's office. They arrested him this afternoon over in Madaga."

I gave her the lowdown on what was happening while she scratched Herk's ears. She sat patiently listening until I was through.

"So let me make sure I've got this all straight," she said. "You got called down to the morgue in Partridgeberry to ID a body they thought was your brother but turned out not to be. Then you find out later it was this doppelgänger criminal from Canada who somehow showed up dead on Bo's doorstep. And now Bo's been arrested and charged with murdering him."

"That pretty much sums it up."

"See. This is why I love working here. This place is like *The National Enquirer* on stimulants. And to think, all I did last night was eat six and a half pieces of reheated pizza, drink three bottles of diet soda, and binge on *Simpsons* reruns."

"I'm sorry. I should've told you about the body yesterday."

"No. No. What I have to do every day here to try to keep this place going can't possibly hold a candle to breathing in some of your exalted wake, Billy. As I'm always telling people, there's nothing like basking in the aura of a professional athlete. All the glitz and glamour. All the attention and the celebrity perks."

"Are you through?" I asked.

"No. I'm *not* through. How could you not come talk to your spirit sister when all this fuddlygrubby, whatever it is, was going down? Maybe I could've helped you head some of this stuff off."

Petula had once attended a two-hour seminar on the horoscope and North American Native American rituals. She'd come away afterward with the notion that she and I were actually of one spiritual mind, along with a few other offbeat ideas. Most of which changed when she started going to church, became friends with Aubrey, and took more of an active role in her faith.

I continued, "Like I said. I'm truly sorry. The last thing I wanted was for you or anybody else to get into trouble. I rely on you to keep things going around here. I appreciate you, and I should've leveled with you."

She glared at me for a moment longer before her face softened. "Apology accepted," she said. "Moving on."

"Thank you."

"How'd you end up with Herk here?"

"Justine's away at some sort of conference. Left on a flight out of LaGuardia first thing this morning. I actually forgot she was going. She was waiting for me with Herk at the cabin when I got home last night."

"She was, huh? Not the best timing. Did you tell *her* what's going on?"

"Not a word. Although, as you say, I'm sure she, like everybody else, will find out soon enough." I pictured Justine enjoying a cocktail and hors d'oeuvres at her conference when someone sprung the news on her. While I hated to admit it, the idea made me feel all warm and fuzzy inside.

"But your ex is a lawyer. Even if she does act like Cruella de Vil."

"Justine would be the last person I'd look to for help with something like this. She's always disliked Bo. Besides, she's not even that kind of an attorney. And, as for having Herk with me, you know I'd keep him full time if she'd ever just say the word. He's been a great wingman so far."

"Okay. Whatever you say." She took out her cell phone. "I'm thinking we still need reinforcements here. I'm contacting Aubrey."

"Aubrey? Hold on a minute," I said.

I pictured our neighborhood baker and her alluring countenance. We seemed to be in the process of developing a connection. Would a dead doppelgänger and Bo's arrest get in the way of that? Anyone who was raising a teen alone after losing their spouse, like Aubrey, had no doubt been through worse, but I didn't want to jinx whatever might be brewing between us. Then again, I'd learned the hard way that any connection that couldn't stand the test of trouble wasn't worth having.

"What's wrong with calling her?"

"Nothing," I said. "I guess I just don't want to start a bunch of rumors."

"I guarantee you they've started already. Everybody in this county will know by tomorrow, if they don't already. Besides, we can trust Aubrey. And she might even be able to help. Her family's lived here for generations. Her grandfather used to be sheriff, you know. He's still sharp as a tack, she tells me."

"Really? I didn't know that," I said.

"Don't worry, Billy. I've got your back." She looked at her phone and fired off a text and apparently received an almost immediate response. "She says she's already heard. And she's willing to help any way she can. Says she'll give you a call."

"Oh, wow. Tell her I appreciate it."

Maybe she could be of help with Sheriff Lawton. Especially if her grandfather had been sheriff a generation before him.

"You know I've been sitting out there at the desk, praying off and on and wondering if something big was going on. One of the guys who came into bowl earlier said something about the TreadBo factory in Partridgeberry being searched today."

"It's true. Bo's assistant, Carianne, said they took his office computer and a bunch of files."

"Well, at least this explains why you've been acting so weird. How'd it go with Fontainebleau? You think he's mixed up in any of this?"

"Maybe. That's why I went to see him. He says Bo borrowed money from him to help keep the factory going."

"You're kidding. That's just what we need. Another dysfunctional political power broker to spice up our lives. If we don't watch out, we're going to be trending on YouTube again. Which is only a good thing if you're one of those teenagers who have their own channels and are said to be making piles of money by having a gazillion subscribers. Although I'm not even so sure that's a good thing either."

"Well, the loan was news to me," I said. "Fontainebleau claims they just closed on the deal. Says he transferred the money last week."

"Transferred it where?"

"I don't know, but according to Bo's assistant, it didn't go into the factory account."

"That sounds fishy." Petula wrinkled her nose. "How much money are we talking about?"

"A half a million dollars."

"Holy moly." She whistled softly. "That's a lot of cash."

I nodded. We had a modest saving plan, a 401k, set up for me and our few employees at Split City. Some years, it was all I could do to scrape together enough money to contribute a meager amount.

"You think Fontainebleau's telling the truth?" she said.

"Maybe. Why would he lie about something like that? Plus, I'm wondering if the dead guy I was called in to identify might have duped him."

She smiled. "Of course. That makes total sense. If he looked that much like you and Bo, he could have gotten away with it."

"True," I said. "But it still remains to be seen."

After all, I was thinking, how could anybody be so stupid as to give a man they thought was someone it wasn't a half a million dollars?

Then again, it might not have been all that hard. Don't we all become so familiar with people around us that we take them for granted? Don't we sometimes fail to see them for who they really are? You throw in the twin aspect, and you throw in the fact that Fontainebleau probably didn't interact with Bo all that often.

If Bouchard knew the right things to say, he could have stolen the right credentials. He could have pulled it off. If I were a local bigwig like Fontainebleau and had half a million dollars to invest in a struggling area business, I might even have given him the money myself.

Petula sat up straight. "Maybe all of this also explains why our local sheriff's deputy has been hanging around here all evening bowling and chatting up customers. You know, 'Mac the Marv' of the marvelous young body. That's what some of older female patrons call him. He must know about Bo's arrest. Maybe he's been assigned to keep an eye on you."

"Great. That's just what I need right now," I said. "I see we're still in business, at any rate. And fairly busy, surprisingly enough." It was true. The lanes looked like they were more than half full. Not too shabby for a weekday night when the summer season was still weeks away.

"Aww, well, I hate to break the news to you, boss... but today's the fundraiser for the Our Lady of the Partridgeberry Shrine committee. Most of these bowlers are non-paying."

From her perch atop one of the surrounding hills, the Our Lady of the Partridgeberry shrine had been looking over the lake and presiding over Twin Strikes for as long as I'd lived there and no doubt many years before. Its history seemed a little murky, but no one seemed to care.

"Plus," she continued, "word must have gotten out on Instagram or something about our hunky Mac the Marv being here. Since he showed up, the number of female middle-aged shrine committee members seems to have doubled."

"Figures," I said, thinking I better not talk to Mac right now. "Is anybody here actually paying to bowl?"

She ignored the question. "But hey, look at all of the great community service we're providing," she said. "At least these lady keepers of the flame will be able to have that shrine's lawn mowed again this summer. And if they scoop up enough cash in that big old collection bucket of theirs, they might even be able to add a few more wooden supports to keep that old mountainside relic from tumbling down into the lake for another year."

"Wonderful. Glad to hear we're doing our part." I looked out absently through the office window at Mac and the other bowlers scattered among the lanes.

"What are you thinking, Billy?" Petula asked.

"I'm thinking I need to get out of here with Herk and try to regroup. I'll know more in the morning when I'm able to have another talk with Bo. I've been hoping I might get a call from his lawyer, but I've heard nothing."

"All right. And don't forget Aubrey's going to call you, too."

"I won't. I don't want to run into Mac on the way out though."

Petula angled her chin with an impish grin as one of her curls draped over her face. "Don't worry," she said. "I'll work on keeping our handsome young deputy busy. The shrine girls can get their fill of Mac eye candy and keep stuffing that bucket of theirs while you and Herk sneak out the back door."

"Sounds like a plan. Should I ask how?"

"No, you should not." She laughed.

# 23

On the way home, Herk and I swung by the grocery store to pick up some more dog food. Things were quiet in the pet supplies aisle. In addition to the food, I couldn't resist a giant chewy stick that seemed to have Herk's name on it.

Back at the cabin, he downed his meal and went to work on the stick. I chewed on a sliced apple while waiting for the frozen TV dinner I had cooking in the oven. My phone buzzed on the counter.

Aubrey.

I took a deep breath and answered. "Hi. Thanks for calling."

"Are you okay?" she asked, sounding genuinely concerned.

I loved that. No assumptions. No preconceived notions about what I was thinking.

"Not really," I said. "I'm sitting her confused, frustrated, and angry. Trying to go over what I know and start to figure out what's going on with Bo."

"I don't blame you. Under the circumstances, those sound like normal emotions."

If I could have reached out through the phone, I would have kissed her.

"I-I appreciate you saying that," I stammered. "And for being willing to help. I hope it's not too much trouble."

"Not at all," she said. "I spoke again with Petula. She went over everything you told her. After that I reached out to my grandfather."

"She said he used to be sheriff."

"That's right. For over twenty years. But that was a long time ago. Most of his contemporaries have passed on by now. He's still sharp and keeps an ear to the ground about what's happening though."

"Did he know about Bo?"

"Of course. The weird dead body and everything. The county only averages a couple of homicides per year, he said. He said he's surprised they made such a fast arrest. They must think they have a good motive or solid evidence."

If I was going to try to help my brother, evidence was something I seemed to be sorely lacking. Why hadn't I heard from his lawyer? I also would've thought Bo had a good alibi being over in Madaga when the killing happened. Sheriff Lawton had to know something I didn't.

"Did you tell him what Fontainebleau told me about the loan?" I asked.

"Yes. And he said that probably has something do with it. Leonard Scriblow is Sheriff Lawton's chief investigator."

"I met him. But what's that got to do with anything?"

"Scriblow's stepson works for Fontainebleau at the resort."

Another new revelation. Was everybody and everything in this town related to one another? I should have known better by now. It might mean something or might mean nothing at all.

"Grandpa doesn't have a particularly high opinion of Fontainebleau," she said.

"Sounds like my kinda guy. I'd love to have a deeper talk with your grandpa some time."

"I'm sure that can be arranged." I pictured her with a smile as she said this.

Because it was a potential connection between us?

"Does your brother have a lawyer?" she asked.

"I can't imagine he doesn't by now. But no one's contacted me. And his administrative assistant at TreadBo doesn't seem to know anything either."

"Grandpa said he'll make some inquiries tomorrow. Judge Carlyle is fair, he said. He said you should know a lot more after the arraignment tomorrow."

"Who's the prosecutor?" I asked.

"Rex Stevens. Old Man Stevens, they call him. Younger than my grandfather, but also seems like he's been here forever."

"Is Stevens a good prosecutor?"

"Grandpa didn't say. But he did say you could trust Sheriff Lawton. He thinks Lawton's a good man."

"Great," I said. "That doesn't exactly bode well for Bo. Who can I not trust?"

"I guess that remains to be seen," she said.

"Did he say anything else?"

"Nope. That's about it for now."

"Thank you again for calling."

"You're welcome. Let me know if there's anything else I can do. And try to get some rest," she said. "You're going to need it."

# 24

I walked into the sheriff's office in Partridgeberry early the next morning.

Glancing back through the glass entrance, I spotted Herk sitting happily in the front passenger seat of my SUV in the parking lot. He'd been a good copilot through all of this. Despite the age and no doubt many smells that had accumulated over the years in my vehicle, he seemed at home in the dunge. I'd left him with his favorite giant rawhide. Sooner or later, he'd lie down and begin to gnaw on it.

I'd only visited the sheriff's office once before, to file a complaint about a drunk and disorderly bowler. The jail, which I'd never been in, was in the back of the building. The rest of the office looked the same now as it did then.

A few cheap plastic chairs on an old linoleum floor greeted people as they walked in the front door. In an open area behind a makeshift reception desk (empty at the moment) four desks formed orderly ranks, each with outdated computer screens. Filing cabinets, a long countertop, and a modern printer and fax machine encircled the rest of the room while blinking security cameras hanging from the ceiling seemed to keep a watchful eye on things. A cracked concrete floor in one back corner led to the block of cells where Bo must have spent the night.

Not exactly the five-star condominium where he was used to residing.

"I see we have a visitor."

To one side of the room stood the sheriff's private office. It had a large picture window with opened blinds. Sheriff Lawton must have caught sight of me through his office window and emerged through its open door.

"Hello, Sheriff. I'm here to see my brother."

"Didn't think you were making a social call," he said. "Haven't you talked to his lawyer?"

"No, I haven't heard from anybody."

"Huh. Well, technically speaking, visiting hours aren't until ten. But, since you're already here and your brother's due to be arraigned in a few hours, I don't see why not."

"I appreciate it. Can you tell me—?"

He held up his hand, silencing me.

"The DA's got your brother's case, and the investigation is ongoing," he said. "Sorry. For the time being, I can't tell you any more than that."

"Have you seen Bo's lawyer?"

"Yes. The man was here until late last night. Some hotshot from Albany. Said he'll be back later this morning for the hearing."

That, at least, was a hopeful sign. I hoped. How much did defense attorneys charge for a murder case? I had no idea.

"Come on," he said. "I'll take you back to see your brother."

I followed the sheriff across the large room. Now it was my turn to look at him with the same sort of investigative detachment he'd been using on me. What I saw was a deep weariness. Murders didn't happen every day in Partridgeberry.

"Where are your deputies?" I asked.

"Most are out on patrol or off duty. Only one stays in the building, and they have to watch the video monitor of the building and cells if we have prisoners in the house. We run a pretty lean operation. Always having to beg the county supervisors for more funding."

I wondered if that gave Fontainebleau, since he had a seat on the county board of supervisors, some kind of outsized power over this situation. Partridgeberry County, unlike its neighbor Madaga, wasn't exactly a hotbed of economic activity. Other than money from the resort and lake tourism, local tax revenues tended to suffer as a result. Which was why the TreadBo factory was seen as a welcome addition to the area.

"Even so," the sheriff added, as if he had to explain himself, "we don't miss much."

Beyond the barred entryway, a corridor led to a more heavily reinforced metal door with a small window made of thick glass toward the top. In front of the door stood a walk-through metal detector.

"You'll have to surrender everything except your driver's license before entering the cell block," Chamber's said. "No phone, of course. No keys or metal of any kind. Not even your wallet. You have any metal implants?"

"Nope," I said.

"All right then."

I emptied my pockets and handed over everything he asked for, and he turned and used a key he pulled from a cord attached to his belt to lock them all in a small safe built into the wall. He invited me to step forward and stood to one side as I walked silently through the metal detector. Then, moving around me, he typed in some kind of a code on a covered keyboard attached to the wall. The door buzzed open.

Passing through it, I caught sight of the cells. There were only six of them. They looked slightly newer than the rest of the building but not by much. Instead of open barred enclosures the cells were behind solid walls, three on either side of a short hallway, with more heavy metal windowed doors. At a desk in the hall sat a female deputy I'd never seen before.

Which was disappointing because I was hoping it would be Scriblow on duty.

"Prisoner's got a visitor. Here on my approval," Lawton said to the deputy. "Name is Billy Gills. He's the prisoner's brother. Could you please enter the information from his driver's license into the log?"

"Sure thing, Sheriff."

She looked to be in her mid to late thirties, and her attention was riveted on a much larger computer screen than the ones out front. She was in uniform, of course, minus her hat, but her belt came stocked with a dark semiautomatic handgun and a Taser that looked much more powerful than the ones I'd seen belonging to the security guards at the casino. In a different light, her lean figure, angular face, and short blonde hair might even have been considered attractive. If she knew who I was, or was surprised to see that I looked almost exactly like her prisoner, she didn't give anything away by her expression.

"All right, Billy. Janet will take care of you from here," Lawton said. He turned and disappeared out the door through which we'd just come.

I handed my driver's license to the deputy, who looked at it, set it along top of the keyboard in front of her, and started typing.

"Okay," she said. "You're all set. First door on the left is the visitor's booth. I'm going to take you in there now. Inside you'll find a chair facing a window with a phone receiver on the wall. Wait there, and I'll bring the prisoner in from the other side. You'll be able to speak to the prisoner through the glass. All conversations are private with no recording other than video monitoring. Visits are limited to thirty minutes. Do you have questions?"

"No, ma'am. That all seems pretty clear."

She ushered me into a plain small room, not much bigger than a closet with a chair and a window on one end. I'm not a fan of small spaces. For a moment I wondered if I was actually the prisoner.

It wasn't long, however, before a door on the other side of the window opened, and the deputy led Bo into what appeared to be an equally small room nearly identical to the one where I sat.

Bo sat there, handcuffed. He'd been forced to shed his street clothes in favor of an orange jumpsuit with PRISONER PARTRIDGEBERRY SHERIFF'S DEPARTMENT stamped in bright, hard-to-miss lettering across the front. The deputy released him from the cuffs and disappeared out the door.

# 25

We stared at one another for a couple of moments. I could only imagine what might be going through his mind. Then Bo picked up the phone handpiece on the wall and put it to his ear. I did the same.

"This is some kind of loony nightmare." His voice sounded thin through the line.

"I'm having a hard time trying to wrap my head around it myself," I said.

"They're charging me with murder, did you know that?"

I nodded.

"They showed me photos from the morgue. This guy they say I killed, like I told you, I never saw him before in my life. Never even heard of the guy. I couldn't believe how much he looked like you and me. Except different. Just like you said."

"When the sheriff and Deputy Scriblow were questioning you before the arrest, did they give you a chance to explain yourself?"

"Not that much. I tried to tell them, but they obviously didn't believe me. They have phone records they say prove I'm lying. They're saying I had a motive—basically stealing money—and that they have video showing I left Madaga that night, which isn't true. They say the dead man was some kind of a criminal from Canada. Seems like they think he was trying to extort money from me, and that I snapped. Or something."

"Did you?" I asked.

"What?"

"Snap."

Maybe it sounded harsh. But I had to ask.

"C'mon, Billy. You know me better than that," he said. "I have no idea what they're talking about. They said they found calls from me to him on my cell phone, but I never made any such calls."

"Didn't you notice the calls on your phone the next morning?"

"No. I don't usually go through my call log after the fact, especially when I'm busy."

"Somebody must have gotten a hold of your phone, then put it back."

"Maybe—they would have had to have broken into my room then and been pretty quiet about it. Because I remember putting it on my bedside table before crawling into bed. It was right there next to me when I woke up. Or maybe they got ahold of my phone some other way. I don't know."

I made a mental note to follow up on this.

"You didn't wake or hear anything in the night?" I asked.

"No. Like I told them, I was out cold. I'm a heavy sleeper to begin with, and I must've had too much to drink at the party."

"How come I haven't heard from your lawyer? How can I help you when I don't know what the evidence is against you?"

"He told me not to say anything right now. To you or anyone else. He says I shouldn't answer any more questions from the police. He said he needs to have a chance to review all of the evidence and the case against me before my arraignment."

"Do you want me to try to help you?"

"Of course. I'll tell you everything I know after the hearing."

"Did the lawyer say what he thought was going to happen at the arraignment or how much bail he thought you were going to have to put up?"

He looked even more downcast. "He said bail's not always so easy to get in a murder case. Even if I have no criminal record, I have money and I'm considered a flight risk. And worse, he said he's dealt with this judge before. Apparently, the man has a reputation for coming down hard in murder cases and also seems bent on making examples out of perpetrators of white-collar crime. Which I guess is what they're also thinking this is because they're charging me with fraud as well."

"What if the judge doesn't grant bail?" I asked.

"My lawyer says he can probably win it on appeal, but it could take time…which means I could be stuck in here for a while."

The gravity of the situation became even clearer. This wasn't some cheap or offhand mistake. It wasn't about to be undone with a few easy steps. Despite our many differences, I didn't believe my twin brother was some kind of a scam artist, let alone a murderer. But, given his eccentricities, I could see to someone else how it might look like he was.

"Let's just take things one step at time," I said. "I have to ask you something."

"What?"

"I knew about the money you lost because of Split Down the Middle of course. But why didn't you tell me about your business being down and the money troubles you've been having with TreadBo?"

"Who told you about that?"

"Giuseppe Rhodes said he suspected TreadBo was having financial problems, and Carianne mentioned it too."

Bo blew out a long breath. "I'm sorry, Billy. I didn't want to burden you with anything more than what you're already trying to manage at Split City. It's just corporate finance stuff, a temporary liquidity issue. The factory has weathered these kinds of things before—"

"Did you borrow money from Max Fontainebleau?"

He tilted his head as if he'd been struck in the face. "Fontainebleau? What are you, nuts? I wouldn't borrow a dime from that opportunist."

"He claims he loaned you and TreadBo a half a million dollars."

"That's insane."

"You should let your lawyer know that. There's something really funky going on here."

"I'll say. How do you know about all of this?"

"Because I've been trying to figure out what's going on. Fontainebleau came by Split City to try to talk to me, but I wasn't there. Then I heard from Carianne he'd been hanging around the factory, that he was there when the sheriff and deputies were searching your office, so I went to confront him. Thing is, I think he might be telling the truth. At least, I think he may have actually given the money to somebody, probably this dead lookalike."

"Wow. Do you think Fontainebleau killed the guy when he found out he wasn't for real?"

"I don't know. What would have been his motive?"

"Maybe he thinks the guy was working with someone and that someone was me. Maybe he thinks I know where his money is."

"That makes no sense at all," I said. *None of it was adding up.* "You're absolutely sure you didn't go anywhere near the TreadBo building the other night?"

"How many times do I have to say it! I was asleep in my room at the hotel in Madaga the whole time."

"Maybe you had a bad reaction to something you ate or drank at that Pontefio hospitality suite. You told me you couldn't quite remember everything that happened."

"Yeah. But I think I would've remembered something if I somehow made it all the way back over here to Partridgeberry. And I specifically remember crawling in between the sheets in my hotel bed that night. I put on my pajama bottoms, but I still had on a sport shirt. I had a headache and stomachache, and I just wanted to close my eyes and go to sleep. I woke up the next morning dressed the same way."

"Maybe someone drugged you," I said.

"I suppose it's possible. And there's another weird thing."

"What's that?"

"I was in my room doing some work before the convention was supposed to open this morning. Just before Sheriff Lawton called me and the Madaga deputies showed up and asked me to follow them over to their office for questioning, my laptop started acting funny."

"What do you mean 'funny'?"

"It blipped out. Just stopped working. I was in the middle of trying to reboot it when the deputies showed up."

"Where's the laptop now?"

"I assume the police have it. I left it in the safe in my hotel room, and after he placed me under arrest, Lawton asked me for the code to get into it. I figured they could get into the safe even if I didn't give it to them, so I told him." He paused. "This is crazy, Billy. I'm stuck here in jail for something I didn't do!" He pounded his fist on the countertop and against the other side of the glass.

A scratchy voice came through an audio speaker overhead. "Hands off of the glass."

The female deputy. She'd been true to her word. We were being watched.

"Don't worry. We'll get it figured out," I said. "Maybe you'll make bail. Let's see what happens at the arraignment."

"You know they searched the TreadBo offices yesterday."

"Yeah. I went by there, and they wouldn't let me in. Then I went back later and talked to Carianne and Zune."

"They must be freaking out. Wondering what in the world is going on. And I can only imagine what the factory folks are thinking. They also said they're searching my condo. I don't know what they think they're going to find."

"Times almost up," came the voice through the speaker again. "Thirty seconds."

"Don't worry. We're going to get this figured out," I said, trying to sound reassuring.

"We need to somehow prove to the sheriff I didn't do this."

"Right," I said. "And the best way is to try to find out who did."

I tried to say something else to Bo, but the phone had stopped working, and I all could do was wave to him as the deputy came and took him away.

A few minutes later, I'd retrieved my belongings and was heading out the door.

Out front, Lawton didn't even look my way as I passed by his office.

# 26

"All rise," the bailiff announced.

As he spoke, a distinguished-looking man in a black robe appeared on a screen hanging from the front wall of the courtroom. We'd all been told by the bailiff beforehand that for an arraignment like this, the judge was going to preside via video link from Poughkeepsie.

We all stood until the judge was seated. The grainy video made it look like the man's gray hair was part of a spider web atop his head. There was a judicial symbol on a wood paneled wall and an American flag in the corner behind him.

"Court is now in session," the bailiff said. "The State of New York versus Mr. Bo Hampton Gills, the Honorable Terrance Carlyle presiding."

Petula had driven down to pick up Herk to take him back to Split City. I was seated in the public gallery behind Bo and his attorney. I didn't often hear Bo's formal middle name mentioned. Hampton was our maternal grandfather's name. Carianne from

TreadBo sat in the row behind me, along with a couple of curious spectators and a reporter whom I vaguely knew from the Partridgeberry *Weekly Gazette*. Sheriff Lawton and Deputy Scriblow, who no doubt knew this already, were also there. They sat across from us in the gallery, expressionless.

After some housekeeping formalities between the judge and bailiff, Partridgeberry County District Attorney Rex Stevens rose from his chair. Old Man Stevens looked ancient enough and tough enough to have built the building himself. He was clad in a modest but impeccably clean three-piece suit. Charcoal gray, it made his starched white shirt and perfectly straight tie stand out all the more.

"If it please the court," he began, "the people are present, and I believe you have a copy of the indictment, along with our brief outlining the evidence against Mr. Gills in more detail."

"Yes, I have the documents, Mr. Stevens. And I've read through both of them," the judge told him.

And so it went from there.

The result of the arraignment was anything but favorable to Bo. The judge asked Bo's attorney to identify himself and his client for the record, which he did. The charges were read. Bo plead "not guilty," and his plea was entered into the record.

Bail was discussed at some length. The judge asked a few questions. Bo's attorney and the prosecutor went back and forth. Ultimately, the judge denied bail over Bo's attorney's forceful but impotent objections. Otherwise, the hearing proceeded in an abbreviated, businesslike manner—a lot less dramatic than I might have expected. Not like you see on TV. The whole affair was over before I knew it. You might've thought Partridgeberry indicted potential murderers every day.

The judge set a trial date for six weeks hence. Bo's head was down, and his posture slumped lower and lower as the hearing wore on. After bail was denied, he seemed to shrink into a shadow of himself.

I glanced behind me toward the end to see Carianne tearing up.

Turning around for a moment, I whispered, "It'll be okay." Although I really wasn't sure it would be.

She pursed her lips and nodded.

At the end of the hearing, we all rose as the judge disappeared from the screen. Bo's attorney whispered something in his ear as a pair of deputies appeared and stepped to either side of him. We stood and watched Bo being ceremoniously frog-walked out of the courtroom in his orange jumpsuit and shackles. I tried to make eye contact with him, but his eyes remained fixed on the floor.

# 27

I was finally able to speak to Bo's lawyer a couple of hours later. Clad in an expensive looking trench coat over a tailored suit and tasseled leather shoes, he was about to climb into a Porsche SUV in the jail parking lot.

I was headed in to see Bo again and didn't know exactly what I should say to the man. I found out later that the attorney—whose name was John Marinella—was from TreadBo's corporate law firm. Carianne had told me he was considered the firm's best criminal defense attorney, and that Bo had had some interactions with the man in the past regarding a minor accident in the factory and a workman's compensation lawsuit.

Catching sight of me, he said, "I saw you in court, Mr. Gills. Remarkable how much you look like your brother." He examined me as if he might a zoo exhibit. "And I've got to say, this is one of the most bizarre cases I've ever heard of."

Maybe the man was so buried in his work he didn't get out much. All he had to do was turn on the evening news.

"Seems like you got steamrolled at the arraignment," I said. "No bail?"

"I know," he said. "I'm sorry. Not much more I could've done. Judge Carlyle seemed like he'd already made up his mind."

"How'd it go in there just now with Bo?"

"Well enough," he said. "I think the prosecution's case has a lot of holes. I'll leave it up to your brother to tell you what he thinks."

"Can you show me what the police have on him?"

"Your brother has copies he can show to you if he wants."

"Have you ever worked a case like this before?"

"What do you mean?" His expression knee-jerked defensiveness.

"Defended someone accused of murder."

"Once," he said. "But I've worked on a number of wrongful death cases, several of which involved criminal charges."

"What does that mean exactly?"

"A wrongful death suit happens when a company or business owner are accused of negligence that leads to someone losing their life. And often this includes criminal indictments as well."

"Okay, I get it," I said. "You're here, and you're expensive, and you're the best attorney my brother could hire on short notice. How'd did that other murder case of yours turn out?"

"The client was acquitted," the lawyer said proudly.

"So it went all the way to trial," I said.

"Yes, of course," the lawyer said.

"I sure hope that doesn't have to happen here. Bo's innocent."

"Yes, well, I'm filing an appeal about the bail, but I can't make the court move any faster. Besides, in cases like this, it's usually better to have enough time to prepare the right defense."

"Better for you maybe."

The attorney stared at me for a minute but offered no retort. "Well," he said finally, "I hope you have a productive visit with your brother."

With that, he opened the door of his already running SUV and lifted his brief case across to the passenger seat to climb in.

"Have a nice day," I said sarcastically. Looking back, I suppose I could have been more charitable.

"You too." Smiling weakly, he stepped up into his vehicle. Without looking back, he closed the door behind him and drove away.

# 28

Bo and I sat on opposite sides of the glass in the joyless light of the prisoner's visitor room. Gone was my twin's usual confident air, his funky brand of cool. Face drawn, eyes vacant—he bore the gaunt look of someone who'd been blindsided and overwhelmed.

"What'd your attorney have to say?" I asked.

He shook his head and sighed. "I don't know, man. He says the case doesn't seem all that strong. He thinks there's a good chance I can beat this. But he also said it's going to take time. I don't know how much longer I can last cooped up in here."

I could sense his pain and growing sense of panic over the claustrophobic confinement to three walls, a bunk, and the steel bars closing in. I needed to say something to try to keep his spirits up.

"We're going to get you out of here. We just need to figure out what really happened."

He pursed his lips and nodded. "The attorney wants to hire a private investigator."

"Did he talk to you about the evidence they have against you?"

"Yeah. He went through the report with me and left me a copy."

He opened a folder in front of him and spent the next few minutes going over it with me. There were some important details and things to be considered. How the scene had been clumsily staged to look like a suicide and the gun wiped clean of prints. Which meant the killer must have been in a hurry. How there was no gunpowder residue found on the victim's hand, which showed he couldn't have fired the gun. He outlined the dead man's criminal history: Etienne Bouchard's Canadian record included a host of minor infractions, possession of drugs, embezzlement, for which he was convicted, and a couple of strongly suspected, though never fully proven, blackmail schemes that seemed to have been quite sophisticated.

Another thing I learned the sheriff hadn't told me was that when Bouchard's body was found, they'd also discovered an apparently hastily scribbled suicide note. Obviously, they now thought the note was fake. They must have thought Bo had written it to try to cover his tracks.

"As far as why they believe I killed the guy," he said, "most of it is circumstantial. They're focusing on motive. They've been digging into the company's finances. They've talked to my bank. And they've detailed a number of pieces evidence for recent financial distress. The worst part and only hard evidence they seem to have is that they say they have a cell phone record showing my phone was used here in Partridgeberry in the middle of the night around the time of the murder. But that's impossible. I was asleep in my hotel room in Madaga."

I could visualize Bo's steel trap mind attempting to sift through the case they had against him. I joined in.

"That's strange," I said. "What number did your phone supposedly call?"

"That's where it gets interesting. The cell phone company says the call went to an unlisted number in China."

"China?"

"Yeah. To them it makes sense. They think I was working some kind of secret deal or scam with this guy Bouchard to move TreadBo's shoe manufacturing over there to save the company. The middle of the night here is the middle of their working day over there. It's no secret that Asia is where most of the shoes in the world are made."

"But you would never do that. Would you?'

"Of course not."

"Could someone have hacked into your phone?" I asked. My mind was abuzz with the possibilities.

"I don't know," he said. "Maybe. The phone's brand-new. I just bought it a few days ago. But the sheriff took it along with my laptop and other belongings."

"Yeah. And the computer from your office at the factory too."

I made a mental note to check into the phone further.

"The bottom line," Bo said, "is that they think I was communicating with this guy Bouchard. That I was in on a scam to bilk Fontainebleau of his money and up to some secret overseas plan. And something went wrong, and so I killed him. They think I am crazy. Lots of people do. I've gotten used to it."

"What about the hotel where you were staying?" I asked. "Wouldn't there be security camera footage showing whether or not you left that night?"

"They claim they have security camera footage from the hotel showing that Bouchard was there at the convention the same time as I was the afternoon before he was killed and that he was there to talk to me. At first, they thought it was you, but they verified you were at Split City all day and into the evening."

It was true. I'd been at the alley all day on Sunday.

"But what about that night?"

"They also say they have footage of me leaving the hotel that night. But the attorney also pointed out that the hotel reported having some problems with their security cameras."

Funny how things can look one way, and certain facts can seem to line up to make an argument. But what if there was an alternative case to be made?

"What if the police are right, Billy? What if Bouchard was there at the convention? Think about it. He had to be there to be able to do something to my phone. He could have passed himself off as me."

"All right. I can check it out," I said. "I'm going to assume you want me to help you in whatever way I can."

"Yes. At this point, I'd say, anything you can do. Just don't go getting yourself into trouble too."

I held out my hands in a gesture of surrender. "Since when has that ever been a problem, little brother? You're the one who's always pulling the crazy stunts."

# 29

TreadBo marketing director Addison Foley lived by himself in one of the newer townhouse developments of Partridgeberry. Since he worked closely with Bo and hadn't been accounted for, I figured it was time for me to pay a social call.

The dinner hour was fast approaching. The parking spaces in front of the adjacent townhouses were filling with newer SUVs and sedans, even a couple of expensive sports cars. I'd found out from Carianne that Foley drove a black late-model BMW. It was parked in front of his unit when I drove up.

I climbed the brick steps between two trimmed boxwoods in planters and rang the doorbell. There was no answer. I tried it again and got the same result.

Carianne had also given me Foley's cell phone number. I stood on the stoop and dialed it. He answered after the fourth or fifth ring.

"Hello?" His voice sounded weak.

"Addison Foley?"

"Yeah."

"This is Billy Gills, Bo's brother."

"Oh, yeah…I think we've met a couple of times. What's going on? I've heard all about Bo and what's been happening from Carianne. This is major league bad for TreadBo."

He was right about that.

"I'd like to talk to you for few minutes if you're feeling up to it."

"Oh. Okay."

"I'm outside your front door. I rang the doorbell, but no one came. Are you home?"

"Yeah. I must've been sleeping. I'm sick. Didn't they tell you?"

"I understand. But if you can spare a few minutes, I'd really like to ask you some questions."

There was a pause. "All right," he said finally. "I guess. Let me throw on some pants, and I'll be down in a minute."

"I appreciate it," I said. "I'll wait."

I had no idea what, if anything, Foley might know. But the juxtaposition of his sudden illness with Etienne Bouchard's appearance and eventual murder was at least somewhat suspicious.

The sound of the door chain lock rattling and being released reverberated through the front door a couple of minutes later. The door was pulled open to reveal Foley standing there in clean blue jeans and a dark T-shirt with flip-flops on his feet.

"Thank you for seeing me," I said. "Sorry to hear you've been sick."

"Yeah," he said. "Must be some kind of a bad cold. Kind of late in the season. But what can you do? You may not want to get too close."

He was a rangy, angular figure with jet-black hair. Tall, maybe six two or six three. I guessed mid-thirties. His nostrils looked red and irritated from blowing his nose. His eyes were puffy. He really did seem sick.

"No worries," I said. "I just want to ask you a few questions."

"You want to come in? I can get you a glass of water or something."

"If I could, please. And don't trouble yourself about the water. This will only take a couple of minutes."

He nodded, opening the door wider to allow me to pass.

Entering the townhouse, I saw that Foley had expensive tastes. There was a pair of Ming vases on a side table inside the foyer, which somehow con-trasted nicely with the polished wooden floor and a posh-looking rug and contemporary living room suite that nicely filled a two-story open sitting area where tall windows looked out toward woods and fields.

"You have a nice home."

"Thanks. Would you like to sit down?" he asked.

"Sounds good." I took a seat on the stylish couch.

He sat across the room from me in a black lacquered rocking chair.

"Has anyone tried to contact you from the sheriff's department?" I asked.

"Yeah." He turned his head away from me and coughed into his elbow. "Yesterday, somebody named Lawton left me a voicemail. Isn't he the sheriff?"

"That's right."

"I haven't called him back yet though. He didn't say what it was about. But Carianne called me two or three times yesterday. She said there was an office emergency, so I called her back. That's when I found out Bo had been arrested. She said it was something about a murder. So I figured that was why the sheriff was calling. I've never heard anything crazier in my life."

"That's partly why I'm here," I said. "You do sales and marketing for TreadBo, correct?"

"Yeah. Pretty much. It's not like we're a real formal corporation or anything. But I've learned a lot about the shoe industry, and I usually have a good idea what works and what doesn't."

"I understand TreadBo's having a cash flow problem."

Foley shrugged. "Not from where I sit. My budget hasn't been cut. Neither has my salary. Bo's hatching some kind of a new plan, although I'm not quite sure what it is yet."

"A new plan, huh. Have you seen any changes in Bo lately? Any difference in the way he's been acting?"

"No. Not really. He's always been a little different. But hey, you should know. You're his brother."

Yeah. I should know. But the sad truth was, I didn't. People often assumed that Bo and I could read each other's thoughts in some kind of detail. Nothing could have been further from the truth. I could maybe sense Bo's emotion better than others. But he still kept a lot hidden inside.

"All I can think is that there is some kind of a massive screwup happening here," he said. "Some kind of a crazy publicity stunt Bo dreamed up that went horribly wrong or something. He's always trying to come up with something completely different."

"What about you?" I asked.

"Me? I just sell the sizzle. Style and image. That's what some people want from their shoes." He turned his head and brought the back of his hand to his face before sneezing loudly toward the far side of the room.

"Sorry to see you're not feeling well."

"Yeah," he said. "Are we done now? 'Cause I just want to drink some herbal tea and get back in bed."

"No problem. Just one last question. You got sick a few days ago. When did you make the decision not to go to the Madaga convention?"

"Actually, since the convention's so close to home this year, Bo and I have been talking for some time about him going with me. Me getting sick just cemented the idea that he would handle it on his own."

"That reminds me," I said, "I went over there and met with Giuseppe Rhodes. What do you know about him?"

"Rhodes?" He laughed. "Don't let any of those big company people at the shoe convention fool you." He pulled a tissue from a box on the table to blow his nose. "For all of his smooth talk, Rhodes is a corporate hyena, just like most of them."

# 30

"We have a rabbit in one of our ball returns," G said.

He'd greeted me just as I was climbing out of my truck at Split City.

"Come again?"

"A rabbit," he said with a note of exasperation as if he were speaking to a distracted child. "The problems I've been telling you about with lane six and why I had to shut it down. There's a rabbit stuck in the ball return."

As if I didn't have enough to worry about right now.

"How do you know for sure it's a rabbit?" I asked.

He went on to explain how he'd found some remnants of fur stuck to one of the balls, had immediately shut down the lane, and, never lacking for thoroughness, had rushed a sample of the fur off to the veterinary school at Cornell for analysis.

I sighed. "All right. What do we need to do to fix it?" Visions of a bankrupting construction project, and not with sugar plums, danced through my head.

"I found a plumber in Oneonta who can help us," he said. "He uses fiber optics."

"Fiber optics."

"Yeah. It's very high-tech. He'll snake a light and camera down the chute to see what we're dealing with. Chances are, the ball return is intact. According to the folks at Cornell, the critter most likely made it into the building somehow, crawled down the return for a nap, and now can't get out. Probably found some kind of little perch in there. Apparently, the high-tech plumber also has a tool he thinks he can use to grab the creature and yank it out of there before it dies, if it hasn't already."

Just what I needed: the death of a rabbit on my hands. I could already feel the guilt rising in my throat.

"So basically, what you're saying is, our ball return needs an emergency colonoscopy."

G smiled. "That's it exactly, boss. Be a lot cheaper than tearing the lane up."

"What about the state environmental people? Don't they work for free?"

"Yeah, but they said they can't get to us for a while. Apparently, they're backed up with work. Of course, they said they want to be on hand when it happens, if they can, to make sure the critter comes to no harm… that is, like I said, if it's not already dead."

*Lord, please give me the strength.*

"Okay," I said. "Call back the guy from Oneonta."

"Don't you want to know how much he charges?'

"Doesn't matter. Just tell him we need him here ASAP. Let's get the rabbit out of there, sanitize the lane and ball return, and if the creature's still alive, turn it over to the environmental folks."

"Roger, Captain," G said. "Launching operation Rabbit Rescue." He was already raising his cell phone to his ear as he scuttled off to head back around the building to the service entrance in the rear.

At least I'd solved one problem for the day—or so I hoped. Now all I had on my plate was a murder to solve.

#

"How'd it go at the arraignment?" Petula asked from behind her perch at the front desk when I stepped in the front door.

"Not good." I gave her a capsule summary.

"Sounds like you have some good leads to follow. Don't worry about work. We've got everything covered here at the alley. I still suspect Fontainebleau's involved. I guess you'll know more tomorrow."

"I appreciate it. You give Herk any dinner?" I kept a stash of canned dog food in my office filing cabinet.

"Sure thing. He wolfed it down like he'd never eaten before."

"Great. The ways things are going around here business-wise, I hope I can continue to feed him."

"Actually, we've had a better night than usual, all things considered. Several folks I hadn't seen in a while came in and bowled a few games. Who knows? Maybe it's morbid curiosity with your brother in jail charged with murder."

"Either that or they feel sorry for us."

"Ah, don't you worry about it," she said, waving away my negativity. "Thank God for small blessings. Big ones too. Things will work out with Bo and this whole thing. You'll see. You just gotta stay focused. Five-step approach. Think perfect pocket shot to find the real killer."

"You make it sound easy."

"It might turn out to be, you know?" she said. "The answer could turn out to be right under your nose."

"Ha. I hope you're right."

"By the way, you said Justine's coming back in a couple of days, right?"

"Uh-huh."

"And you're supposed to give Herk back when she comes."

"Yes."

She wrinkled up he nose. "Well, I say tell that conniving little two-timer you can't share the dog right now. You need Herk with you. He's providing good solace for you with what you're going through."

"Solace?"

"Yeah. You know. A comforting presence," she said.

Maybe she was right. A comforting presence was exactly what I needed right now.

#

It was nearing dusk by the time Herk and I got home. Shadows reached under the trees and out into the lake below the house. A dark gray fog hovered out across the water.

I took Herk for a short walk, then went into the cabin. Turned on all of the lights and went through the motions of making and eating my dinner.

I tried to take some notes about everything I'd learned. But none of it made much sense so far. I watched some TV to clear my mind but could find nothing that grabbed my attention and soon gave up.

I turned the ringer off on my phone and, dropping headlong into bed, fell into a deep sleep.

# 31

On occasion, Max Fontainebleau could be found behind his desk in the administrative offices of the sprawling Lake Conostowakaka Resort. I went to look for him there and got lucky.

"Do you have an appointment, Mr. Gill?" His secretary, an older woman with a schoolmarmish demeanor, attempted to stare me down.

"Nope," I said. "But Mr. Fontainebleau has a half a million reasons to see me right now."

I didn't stop as I passed by her desk. Just kept going. I had no time to waste. Plus, I didn't want to leave Herk alone in the truck any longer that I had to.

Out of the corner of my eye, I saw her pick up her office phone, put it to her ear, and push a button, no doubt attempting to warn the boss. But I was already through the heavy wooden door to Fontainebleau's office and closing it behind me.

Inside I found our questionable county supervisor lying back with his eyes closed in the reclining position of his executive chair. One of his hands was outstretched. Next to him on the floor knelt a young Asian woman. She was doing his nails.

"Good day, Max. Nice to see you looking so…fit this morning."

Fontainebleau's eyes flew open. Jerking his hand away from the manicurist, he struggled a bit as he sat up in the big leather chair. "I'll poke your eye out, Gills. You know better than to go barging in on a man like this."

"My apologies. But you know I'm getting kind of desperate to see the truth come out about my brother and get him out of jail."

"Yeah, well, maybe you should be desperate. Because, if you ask me, your twin brother's right where he belongs." With a flick of his hand and a side nod of his head he shooed the woman away.

She quickly gathered up her things and, without looking at me, exited the room.

I waited until the door closed behind her.

"My brother didn't bilk you out of that money, Max. He didn't even know about it. You got scammed by an imposter. The guy who's now dead."

"Oh, yeah? So you say."

"Yeah. And what I really think is that you already figured that out," I said, trying to reason with him. "Do you really think my brother would come to you, of all people, for money?"

He shrugged. "You just said yourself you're desperate. Seems to me like your brother is desperate too. Desperate for cash. Desperate to keep his company from going bankrupt. I got a source in the prosecutor's office. Way I hear it, he and this criminal lookalike were in cahoots. First, they bilked me out of my dough, then they were planning to do some deal with the Chinese, probably shutter the TreadBo factory in Partridgeberry and lay off all of the American workers. You know part of my job as supervisor is to protect jobs around here, and I—"

"Let me stop you right there," I said. "That's a fantasy, and I'm going to prove it. Seems to me you're ignoring the fact that the guy who actually took your money is now lying dead in the morgue. The more obvious conclusion is that you found out he stole from you and had him killed."

He stared at me long and hard. Then he reached for his side drawer, and for a moment, I thought he was about to pull out a gun. But instead, he lifted out a fat cigar, which he stuck between his teeth. "I'll say this for you, Gills," he said between his teeth, "you've got a lot of cajones walking in on me this morning and continuing to try to accuse me. Especially after I tried to help you out by giving you the lead on that shoe executive Rhodes. How do I know you're not partnered with your brother in this whole scam?"

"How do I know you're not sending me off on a snipe hunt? You could be just trying to cover your tracks. Maybe you're just trying to pin this murder on Bo to keep the authorities from focusing on you as a potential suspect."

He smiled. "I don't have to defend myself to you, my friend. And don't forget, I'm still your landlord."

"Did you, or did you not, have Etienne Bouchard killed?"

"Absolutely not. What do you take me for?"

I thought about it for a few seconds. Then I said, "You're a bully. A smart and enterprising bully, I'll give you that. But I don't like bullies, landlord or not. You may not have had Bouchard killed. Or you may have. Either way, I'm going to find out who did it."

I turned to go.

He chuckled, chomping down on his cigar before removing it from his mouth. "Like I said, you've got some brass, Billy Gills. Let's see if you can back it up. But if I were you, I'd be focusing on something else."

"Yeah? What's that?" I said, looking back as I opened the door to leave.

"That you may not know this identical twin brother of yours as well as you think," he said.

# 32

I was happy to let Fontainebleau have the last word. For now.

Driving back through town with Herk in the co-pilot seat, it occurred to me that I might've made a mistake, however, avoiding our local Deputy Mac Mallen a couple of nights before. I needed someone on the inside of the sheriff's department investigation into Etienne Bouchard's death. Lawton and Scriblow had seemed very interested in talking to me about the body two days ago. But since they'd arrested Bo, I'd apparently become persona non grata.

I dialed the main alley number in Twin Strikes.

Petula answered in a variation of her usual cheery voice—the sing-song version she mainly reserved for customers.

"It's me," I said.

"Billy?" Her voice dropped to a conspiratorial whisper. "How's the investigation going?"

"It's going. Did Mac Mallen say anything to you the other night before he left?"

"No. I think he got tired of the old ladies ogling him. I heard one of them say he was going home. Said she wouldn't mind tagging along with him. Those shrine ladies are shameless. Why? You want to talk to Mac now?"

I swear sometimes Petula was a mind reader. "Yeah, maybe," I said.

"I think it's his day off."

"Thanks. Good to know."

#

The morning was wearing on with a swirl of gray clouding the sky overhead. Mac Mallen lived in a small house that stood alone along the highway midway between Partridgeberry and our lake town. His county cruiser was parked in the driveway. I'd barely started to climb out of the 4Runner when I saw him swing the front storm door open and poke his head out.

"I can guess why you're here. And I really can't talk to you," he said.

"It's your day off though, right?"

He folded his arms across his chest. "Yeah. So?"

"C'mon, Mac. You know me. And you know Bo. Something doesn't smell right about this whole situation."

He was dressed in blue jeans and a heavy long-sleeve shirt. As usual, his long black hair was tied back in a ponytail. His eyes scanned up and down the highway, which was thankfully empty at the moment.

Then he sighed. "All right. Pull your truck around behind the house so nobody sees you. I'll let you in the back door."

I did as he asked. In back of the house there was a bright-orange kayak, a workout bench with some serious weights, and a black late-model Harley-Davidson Dyna Wide Glide motorcycle Mac must have just pulled out from winter storage.

He held the back door open for me and Herk.

"Okay if Herk comes in, too?"

"Sure," he said. "Just don't cost me my job, Billy."

"All I want to do is talk."

He said nothing as we entered the kitchen, which was barely big enough for a small table and a couple of chairs. A small set of windows looked out on the woods. He closed the door behind us. "Have a seat. I'd offer you something to drink, but I'm out of everything except water and carrot juice. Wasn't expecting any company."

I pulled out a chair, and he pulled out his and sat down across from me. Herk took up position sitting next to me. I said nothing for a moment, gently scratching the retriever's neck. I hardly knew where to begin.

"It's a whack to the system, I know," Mac said, "when someone close to you is arrested. Especially like this.

I've been with the department for seven years. This is only the second or third murder we've had in all that time. Guy who looks like you and Bo? Creepy situation, if you ask me."

"You probably know by now the sheriff called me in to identify the body two days ago, thinking it was Bo," I said. "They initially told me it was a suicide."

"Of course. But the sheriff suspected right from the beginning it was a murder."

"I found out there was a suicide note."

"Yeah. Obviously a fake," he said. "Not a very good one either, from what I hear."

"The sheriff must have suspected me too at first because he didn't tell me everything." Which interested me almost as much as it bothered me.

"Of course, he didn't tell you everything." He looked at me for a long second. "Think about it for a minute. Any time there's a murder, the first people they look to as potential perps are close relatives. Crappy part is, most people who are killed actually do get done in by someone they love. Or think they love anyway. But you can relax. I don't think they really ever considered you a suspect. Looks like Bo did it."

Even Mac seemed convinced of my brother's guilt.

"But that's just crazy," I said. "There's no way Bo hooked up with some Canadian criminal to pull off some scheme."

"What can I say?" He shrugged. "You'd be surprised at some of the crazy stuff we come across in this job. Maybe not murder all the time. But a lot of other things."

"What do you know about the dead man? Lawton said he was from Quebec and had a criminal record."

"I saw the sheet on him from Canada. Looks like a pretty bad hombre. Probably into way more than what he was ever convicted for."

"And what about Bo's cell phone? Bo said they have record of his phone being in Partridgeberry and not in Madaga the night of the murder."

"Can't confirm that or deny that."

"But there's no way Bo's phone could have been there. Bo said he was asleep in his hotel room and had his phone with him."

He shook his head. "I don't know what to tell you."

"Well, Bo also told me they have security video recording of Bouchard being at the convention in Madaga where Bo was earlier in the day."

"Can't confirm that or deny it either."

"All right. Well, assuming there is such a recording, isn't it possible he was at the convention without Bo's knowledge?"

He made a face. "I suppose so."

"What if Bo wasn't actually in Partridgeberry that night? What if Bouchard somehow got hold of Bo's phone at the convention and tampered with it."

He thought about it for a moment. "You know, sometimes criminals will either steal or hack into somebody's phone number and clone it."

"What does that mean?"

"They get the special code the phone number uses and create a duplicate and sell them to others to make free calls. The charges will all be billed to the cloned number. You didn't hear this from me, but there was one odd little thing they found with Bouchard's body. Scriblow was telling me about it."

"What was that?"

"A cell phone battery. Bouchard was using a burner phone. No surprise there."

"Yeah, I know what that is. It's a temporary phone with preloaded minutes anybody can buy at a store. It isn't tied to any kind of cell phone billing or record of the person buying it if they pay cash."

"Exactly. Crooks use them all the time."

"Regular people do too sometimes." I was thinking of people with bad credit or little money, not to mention tech-savvy teens attempting to hide things from their parents.

"Right, but why have an extra battery for the phone? There was already a battery in the burner phone he was using."

"Can they trace the serial number on the second battery?"

"Maybe. I think they're working on it. You know, just to make sure they tie up all of the loose ends. But hey, listen, I've already told you too much. Like I said, you didn't hear any of this from me. I have a pretty good life being a deputy, and I'd like to keep it that way."

"Understood," I said. "You're a fan of Sheriff Lawton, aren't you?"

"You betcha. Man's been almost like a father to me. Got me straightened out and set me up with this job. Saw something in me back when I wasn't able to see it for myself."

"The sheriff's always struck me as honest. I'm counting on that right now," I said.

"You really believe your brother's innocent, don't you?"

"I do."

"Well," he said. "For what it's worth, I hope you're right."

# 33

My phone rang as I was leaving Mac's place. Looking at the number on the display, my heart sank.

"What's this I hear about your brother being in jail?" an all-too-familiar voice said when I answered.

"Don't worry, Justine," I said. "Bo's situation isn't going to be a corrupting influence on our dog."

"It sounds like more than a situation. They're charging him with murder. And they're saying he killed someone who looks like you guys? What in the world's going on back there?"

"It's complicated."

"Everything is complicated with you, Billy."

I took a deep breath. The last thing I wanted to do right now was start another skirmish with Justine. It had been bad enough when I found out she'd been cheating on me. Since our breakup, we'd managed to come to some measure of peace—especially when it came to caring for Herk.

"Don't worry." I tried to sound reassuring. "I'm sure Bo is innocent. It'll all get sorted out."

"Yeah, well, it better," she said. "You forget I'm an attorney. Sorting things out usually means they get even more complicated."

"Right. Thanks for the encouragement," I said, unable to resist the temptation to get a small dig in.

"Oh, forget it," she said. "I'll be back by the end of week, and I sure hope you're taking good care of our Hercules."

"Our Hercules is happily munching on his chew toy, sitting right here in the seat across from me."

Her harrumph was audible, even from three thousand miles away.

"Goodbye, Billy," she said.

I turned the truck toward Madaga.

"Sorry for the bumps, buddy," I said to Herk, as we jolted over a pothole a little way down the road.

The old springs on the dunge failed to cushion the bumps from the winter frost and ice damage to the highway. It would be summer before the state highway crews finished making all the repairs.

I stopped at a wayside before arriving in Madaga. Herk and I took a short walk up an abandoned trail to enjoy the mountain views and let him relieve himself.

By the time I got to the casino and convention center, the afternoon gambling traffic had already begun to clog the parking garage. I found an open parking space in an outdoor lot and got out Herk's leash and the fake service dog vest I'd used with him before.

But as soon as I started to put it on him, he started to whimper.

"What's the matter?" I asked.

He looked at me forlornly.

"Fine time for you to develop a conscience."

He still looked at me.

"All right. All right. Forget the vest. I'll find some other excuse for getting you into the casino."

I stepped out of the truck and went around to the passenger door and opened it. I reached in and snapped the leash on his collar. Normally, as soon as I did, Herk would bound down from the seat and step along beside me. But not today. He refused to budge.

"Now what?" I put my hands on my hips and looked at him.

He whimpered and turned away from me to stare straight ahead.

"What? You don't like this place or something?"

He still refused to move. Then I saw the problem. I realized he was staring at a billboard across the street advertising a local campground. A photo in the ad showed a family playing with a golden retriever.

"Okay, I get it. You have yourself an imaginary girlfriend."

Herk continued to stare.

It's okay to dream, I guess.

I didn't like the idea of leaving him alone for too long. Nor did I feel like wrestling him out of the seat.

I looked across the lot toward the small booth where I would need to pay for the parking. Inside sat a young man, who couldn't have been more than eighteen, staring out at me. I cracked the widow a little and shut and locked the door. Leaving a perfectly happy Herk behind, I made a beeline for the booth.

"It'll be five dollars for the first four hours," the young man told me through his little window.

"Okay. I don't think I'll be here that long, but here you go." I took two five-dollar bills from my wallet and handed him one. "And there's another five in it for you if you'll keep an eye on that dog in the truck over there while I'm inside."

"Sure thing, mister. No problem."

# 34

I entered the main gaming floor via an ornate ground-level lobby entrance. The casino wasn't exactly Las Vegas but had the same sort of ambience. A smoky aura of angst and risk filled the air. A siren call for those hoping to win against the odds.

Looking around, I spied an empty reception desk. An electronic board listed all of the day's events along with scrolling updates and promotions. The shoe convention was still prominently featured. Checking the times, I noted the convention was scheduled to come to an end with a late luncheon in the grand ballroom scheduled for two o'clock.

The final morning sessions had already ended. Through an open door across the way, I could already see workers beginning to pack up the displays on the convention floor.

Rather than wait until the luncheon, I decided the best opportunity to surprise Rhodes was the Pontefio hospitality suite, which Bo had told me was on the top floor of the hotel. Riding up the elevator with a couple of convention goers, I did my best to remain inconspicuous.

The doors opened on the top floor to laughter and rap music coming from down the hall. From a sample bowling alley soundtrack, I'd rejected in favor of another, I recognized Logic's song "Homicide" featuring Eminem playing in the background.

*You got to be kidding,* I thought. *I couldn't make this stuff up if I tried.*

The door to the suite stood open. More than fifty people had crowded inside, all standing around and talking, drinking wine or coffee or other beverages. Most paid me no mind, but a few cast awkward glances my way.

I didn't spot Rhodes at first. Instead, I noticed a young man in slacks and a T-shirt staring at me from next to the beverage table. He had curly dark hair and wore thick eyeglasses that looked like they'd been expensively made. I'd only edged a little way farther into the room when he walked up to me. He obviously recognized me.

"You must be Billy Gills," he said.

"Good guess."

He laughed and stuck out his hand for me to shake, which I did. "We spoke the other day on the phone."

"Right." I remembered his voice. "You told me where I could find Giuseppe."

"Good deduction," he said. "I was sorry to hear about your brother."

"Yeah, well. We're trying to get it sorted it out."

"A lot of people here have been talking about it. I assume you're here to see Giuseppe."

"You got it."

"He's over there in the corner." He gestured with his heard toward the back of the room, where Rhodes was leaning against a credenza, holding a bottle of beer and talking to an attractive blonde in blue jeans and a tight-fitting sweater.

"Thanks," I said, making a beeline toward the CEO.

Rhodes didn't acknowledge me until I was almost right in front of him. "Oh." He looked up at me with a start. "Oh, my gosh, look who's here. Billy. What a surprise. What brings you back here?"

"Sorry to interrupt," I said. "But it's important. Can I have a word with you in private?"

The music grew louder with the start of the next song. He placed his free hand behind one ear to indicate he hadn't heard me.

"We need to talk," I said, louder this time.

"Of course. Of course," he said.

He leaned toward the woman in the T-shirt, who also leaned toward him, cupped his hand over the side of his mouth, and whispered something unintelligible. She glanced at me with what seemed a mixture of curiosity and surprise, then turned and waded into the crowd, looking for someone else to talk to.

Rhodes directed me toward a door behind him, indicating I should follow him.

On the other side of the door, a palatial bedroom featured a couch with two wing chairs. The noise level dropped considerably as he closed the door behind us.

"Is Bo doing okay?" he asked. "I heard he's in jail for some kind of crazy murder. I've been doing my best to make excuses for him here, but you know how fast rumors can spread."

"Bo's hanging in there. He isn't guilty, of course."

"I'm sure of it. Poor Bo. Here. Have a seat. I still can't believe all this is happening."

We sat down across from one another.

"When we spoke yesterday, you mentioned something about Bo's having financial difficulties with the company," I said.

"Yes."

"Do you know who Max Fontainebleau is?"

He let out a snort of disgust. "I don't know him *personally*. But I know who he is. He's down there in Partridgeberry County where you guys are, owns a bunch of property, from what I understand. I hear he's invested in some companies too. A small but noisy shareholder. Why do you ask?"

"He's apparently made an investment in TreadBo. Or at least he seems to believe he did."

I was fishing here and didn't want to give him too much bait.

"If you don't mind my asking, what's your interest in TreadBo?" I asked.

"TreadBo? It's been a nice line for us. One of several, actually. But I'm afraid it's been eclipsed by other types of shoes of late. I've told Bo more than once he needs to try to spruce things up, maybe come up with some new models or something. But there's only so much I can do."

"Pontefio has no interest in acquiring the company? Max Fontainebleau suggested Pontefio might be angling to take over TreadBo."

"Ah," he said with a swat of his hand. "Rumors. If Fontainebleau had half a brain, he'd know that we have little to no interest in companies like TreadBo."

"How's Pontefio's stock doing these days?" I asked.

"We're holding our own, despite the recent downturn in the market. And the stock market will turn around. It always does. The public markets are high stakes. It's not always easy to keep investors happy."

"I wouldn't know."

"Well"—he raised a beer bottle in my direction and took a swig from it—"count yourself lucky in that regard, my friend. But what's any of this got to do with Bo?"

"I was wondering…," I said. "Did you see anything odd or unusual during the day or during the party or where you last saw Bo?"

"Not really, no. I'm sorry. Bo and I were on another panel that afternoon. I wish I could tell you more," he said.

I remembered the security camera footage of Bouchard being here at the convention the afternoon before he was murdered. "This panel you were on. Bo would have had to leave the TreadBo booth empty while he attended it."

"Of course."

"Did you see him doing anything strange?"

"I don't think so. Although I do remember he was without his cell phone. He said he'd been talking with someone at his TreadBo booth and forgot about the panel until the last minute. He left in such a hurry that he left it behind on a shelf. I only remember because he seemed anxious about it when I saw him. But later he texted that he'd found the phone."

So, Bo's cell phone had been left unattended in the booth for a time. Could Bouchard, or someone else, have tampered with Bo's phone during this time? How would they have known it was there? Unless they were somehow tracking him.

The sheriff's department might also be able to match the time on the convention security camera footage with the time Bo and Rhodes were together on the afternoon panel. Maybe a deeper look at the information from Bo's cell phone provider would offer some clues as well. I could at least bring up the possibility with the sheriff. If I was right, it still wouldn't prove who killed Bouchard. But it would throw a monkey wrench into one of the major pieces of evidence against Bo.

"All right," I said. "I think that's all I need from you right now. Thank you."

I still didn't know if I could trust Rhodes. Could he have somehow been involved? But then, why would he tell me about the phone?

"Absolutely," he said. "Please let me know if there's anything else I can do. Bo has good legal representation I presume."

"Yes. Apparently good enough."

"Well, let me know if he needs more help. I have a few legal people I can contact."

*I'll bet you do,* I thought.

# 35

Whatever Fontainebleau's wild-eyed fantasies might have been, Rhodes appeared to be telling the truth. At least in part. More importantly, I now had a plausible line on how Bouchard may have tampered with Bo's phone.

Back in the truck, I waved to the parking lot attendant who gave me a thumbs-up. Herk seemed fine: tail wagging like crazy as I climbed in and none the worse for the wear.

I called Sheriff Lawton's number. It went to voicemail. I left a message asking him to call me as soon as possible.

Then I started the truck and headed back toward Partridgeberry County.

#

Ninety minutes later, I strode down the sidewalk leading into the sheriff's office in Partridgeberry with Herk on his leash, padding happily along at my side. Sheriff Lawton was just coming out the front door.

"Glad I ran into you, Sheriff," I said. "I left you a voicemail a little while ago asking you to give me a call."

"Whatever it is, it will have to wait, Billy. I'm late for a meeting with the county planning commission. You're not thinking about bringing that dog in here, are you?"

"C'mon, Sheriff. My twin brother is in jail for murder."

Lawton gave me a hard look. "All right," he said with a sigh. "But he stays with the deputy out front. No animals in back near the cells."

"Scout's honor," I said. "And oh, by the way, I think your murder victim tampered with Bo's phone at the convention."

"What are you talking about?"

"I'm just suggesting you need to look into the whole phone thing a little closer."

He looked at me and grunted.

But he didn't say to forget it. He turned his back on me, climbed into his unmarked cruiser, and sped off to wherever he was going.

#

The deputy who'd been monitoring the cells the day before sat alone behind a desk in the main office. Before she could say anything about Herk, I said, "The sheriff just okayed me bringing the dog in here as long as I left him with you. I'm here to visit my brother."

"What, I'm your dog sitter now? Like I've got nothing better to do," she said.

"Just for a little while. I need to talk to Bo. You can call Lawton to double-check if you'd like."

She sighed. But then she shrugged. "Don't worry about it. Looks like a nice enough dog. Might help break up the monotony of being stuck for the day in the office."

She took me back to the cells, where another deputy checked me in to see Bo.

Same sterile room. Same window between us with the phone receiver hanging on the wall for talking to prisoners.

I told Bo about what Fontainebleau and Mac Mallen said and what I'd discovered talking to Rhodes. He mostly sat and listened, nodding his head from time to time, although he seemed to perk up a little with the revelation about the time of his panel and the idea of a better way to prove Bouchard may have tampered with his phone.

"I'm still a little suspicious of Rhodes," I concluded. "Maybe he's trying to make a play to take over TreadBo."

Bo seemed to be considering this idea. "You know things can get pretty strange when you're in business. Allies can become enemies, and enemies can sometimes become friends." A pause. "There's something I haven't told you yet."

I was curious, but not surprised. Bo wasn't exactly an ace at telling me things, let alone baring his soul.

"What's that? You'd kill for some grilled salmon right now?"

I was trying to lighten the mood, but in the stark reality of the jail, it seemed to make no difference.

His expression turned grim. "It might be important to get me out of here."

"All right," I said. "I'm listening."

He sighed and glanced up at the video camera on the ceiling before looking back at me. "You're the first person I've told, so it's confidential. No one at TreadBo even knows what I'm about to tell you."

"Of course." I was afraid he was about to admit to me he was selling out the company and moving the plant overseas or something, like others had suggested. Now he had me leaning forward toward the glass.

"I've been secretly working on some new designs for TreadBo shoes," he said.

"Okay," I said. "Is that all?"

New TreadBo designs didn't exactly seem like such a huge revelation. The company had been struggling of late. Even Rhodes had something needed to be done to "freshen up" TreadBo's line of specialty shoes.

"Why keep this from everybody?" I asked.

"Because…" He paused. "The fact that whoever used my number called someone in China the night of the murder is a huge red flag for me. China manufactures more shoes than any other country in the world. Legitimate, licensed brands. And counterfeit brands."

"You're afraid someone's trying to rip off your new designs before you can bring them into production and put theirs out at the same time you do."

"Exactly."

I thought about for a second. "How much do you think those new designs might be worth?"

He rubbed at three days' worth of beard on his chin. "Hard to say. It's purely speculation, but I would guess maybe a couple of million. Maybe more. Overseas counterfeit TreadBos have significantly hurt our foreign sales. Until we're able to shut them down, which we've been able to do, most of the time. We've spent a lot of money defending our trademark and brand. That's mainly what Marinella and his law firm have been doing for us these past few years."

What Etienne Bouchard may have been up to came into clearer focus then. If the Canadian had illicit foreign partners and they thought there were huge sums to be made in illegal manufacturing, they might have bankrolled his activities. But why risk scamming Fontainebleau out of money?

My guess was Bouchard had acted on his own when it came to Max Fontainebleau. If he'd been stalking Partridgeberry County and tracking Bo's computer and Bo, maybe he somehow found out who Fontainebleau was. Maybe he did his homework, and he spotted an opportunity. He wanted to make sure he got a healthy sum for all of his trouble even if things didn't work out with the overseas people.

"You think Bouchard was after your shoe designs," I said.

"Well, it only makes sense, doesn't it?"

"Tell me more about how you've managed to keep the designs secret."

Bo went on to tell me he created the designs only on special drawing paper and not in any digital form. The paper sheets were locked away in a safe in his office at the factory, along with a couple of expensive watches, and five thousand dollars in cash. He asked me to go check and make sure they were still there.

"But the sheriff's department has already searched your office and the factory with a warrant," I said. "Wouldn't they have been able to gain access to the safe and taken whatever was in there as evidence? They might even be stored here somewhere in this building."

He shook his head. "I doubt they would've found the safe." He described how it was hidden away beneath the floor in a corner of his office, told me how I could get into it, and gave me the combination.

"All right," I said. "I'll head over there after the factory closes for the day and see what I can find." Carianne had given me a key card so I could enter the building on my own.

Bo slumped in his chair. Our visiting time was coming to end.

"What's wrong?" I asked.

"What if none of it matters? What if the charges against me go to trial? Who knows what might happen then?

"Don't worry," I said. "Either way, I'm not going to stop until I find out who killed the guy."

I tried to sound more confident than I felt.

\#

Later that afternoon, all was quiet at the TreadBo factory. Whoever might still have been working had apparently gone home for the day. I cruised through the lot, making sure no one else was around.

I used the key card and entered the building without a hitch.

Outside the entrance to Bo's office on the second floor, however, two strips of yellow tape covered the door. Written on them were the words DO NOT ENTER. BY ORDER OF PARTRIDGEBERRY COUNTY SHERIFF'S DEPARTENT.

*Great.*

I looked around, then slipped under the tape and went inside.

Was I breaking some law? Probably. On the other hand, it was my brother's office. Plus, the sheriff's department had already searched this place for evidence. How bad could my crime be?

It was dark inside the office. I didn't want to turn on any lights, so I used the flashlight from my phone to see what I was doing. Fortunately, I was familiar with the layout of the room and knew right where to go to find the concealed safe Bo had told me about.

I found the safe, just as Bo had described. It looked undisturbed. I punched in the electronic combination Bo had given me and pulled open the door, expecting to find the contents Bo had described.

But the safe was empty.

# 36

Operation Rabbit Rescue commenced at 0900 hours the next morning. G introduced me to our plumber, a young man with curly hair and freckles who looked barely older than twenty, almost young enough to be my son. I hoped G knew what he was doing.

What I hadn't anticipated was a reporter from a local news channel who'd showed up with a cameraman, and a group of kids from the local elementary school. Apparently, someone from the state environmental department had leaked that there was another potential problem at Split City. After the debacle of the Split Down the Middle conference, I guess someone thought there might be another story. I wasn't sure how the schoolkids had heard about our rabbit problem. Maybe some well-meaning teacher knew somebody, had heard about it, and thought the occasion might make for an interesting field trip. The fact that some of the kids' parents regularly hunted rabbits to make Brunswick stew must not have occurred to her.

Now everyone wanted to see this little rabbit rescued.

I took G aside and whispered under my breath, "I thought we were supposed to keep this low key."

"What can I say?" he whispered back, shrugging. "It's a small town."

"But what if the rabbit is…you know…?" I made a subtle slashing gesture across my throat, trying not to be too obvious in front of the kids. But how do you slash your throat subtly? I just hoped everyone was focused on the young man as he went to work.

"Don't worry," G reassured me. "Petula's already spoken to the teacher. The teacher's going to keep them all back in the viewing area away from the lane. Only our man here can see the screen, and if it turns out bad, we're supposed to give her a signal. Apparently the teacher already has a story to tell the kids. Something like, 'It turned out to be nothing'. And then she's going to take them into the arcade to distract them."

"All right," I said. "And the reporter?" I sensed another Split Down the Middle-type news disaster brewing.

"Petula's been talking to him. She told him the last thing we need right is negative publicity. She knows him and says he's a nice-enough guy. He's agreed that if this doesn't turn out to be a feel-good story, he'll delete any footage, and forget about it."

I nodded. "Where are the environmental protection people?"

No doubt my nervous tick was starting to twitch.

Again, he shrugged. "They said they're running late. Something about a horse and a cow stuck in a bog."

"Okay." Well, that was one less worry, at least.

I would have to cut out early myself to make it to the jail visiting hours in Partridgeberry to give Bo the bad news about the safe.

"I sure hope this works," I whispered. "The last thing we need right now is another bad viral internet video."

But before I could turn around, our young hired gun had opened up his laptop computer, set it on the top of the return beside the lane, and using stiff wire, had begun to snake a couple of skinny cables down the dark cavity of the ball return.

"Here we go," G said under his breath.

A hush came over the assembled crowd.

I looked up to see Petula approaching from the front desk. I found out later she and the teacher had also devised a simple signal in case the rescue turned into a dead body retrieval.

The young man stared intently at his screen. He'd wisely shielded it from the side in such a way that even G and I couldn't see what he was seeing.

He kept going with the cable. And kept going. Then he stopped.

I held my breath.

The young man scratched his unshaven face. He looked up at G and me and smiled.

"Looks like we got ourselves a cute little bunny staring out at us," he said out loud, turning the screen so we, and all of the onlookers, could see the clear image of a furry face and whiskers and a pair of bright eyes shining in the light from the camera.

The second graders erupted in cheers. The reporter and the TV cameraman with his film rolling moved in a little closer. Applause came from all around.

"Now how are we going to get him out of there?" G asked, again muttering under his breath.

"Don't worry," the young man told us. "I've got a plan."

The plan consisted of a small cage baited with rabbit food. It was open on one end with a trap door. Somehow, the man was able to slide it down the ball return using a flexible but sturdy tube. He slid the cage near the rabbit, and the rabbit went for the food. He gently pulled on a cable, and the door shut. Then he slowly extracted the cage from the tunnel.

As the cage with the bunny neared the opening, squeals of excitement and joy emanated from all around. The TV cameraman captured it all. The rabbit, seemingly oblivious and blinking in the bright light, happily munched away on what must have been its first meal in some time.

It was good timing too. A state environmental agent happened to walk in the front door right at that moment. Just in time to take safe custody of the little lost creature.

"How much do we owe you?" I asked the young man as he was packing up his things to leave.

"Nothing," he said.

I looked at him. "What do you mean, nothing?"

"I've already talked to the TV station people," he said. "If this turned out well, they said they're going to feature me and my business in their story. Best free advertising I've ever gotten."

"Smart," I said. "Thank you."

He packed up to leave, and we shook hands. The enterprising young plumber made sure the reporter caught that on video as well. I could already see the YouTube headline: "Hero Plumber Rescues Rabbit."

Who knew? Maybe fame and fortune were in the wind.

# 37

My spirit buoyed by the success with the rabbit, I was headed out the door for the jail in Partridgeberry when Petula stopped me.

"Can I talk to you for a second?" she said.

"Just for a second," I said. "I'm trying to figure out what's going on with Bo's situation and need to go visit him again."

"Of course." She said she wanted to talk to me about the next Jesus Spares event, scheduled for later that month.

I was just about to ask her to wait to talk to me about it later when an image flew into my head. Not a pretty picture either. It was the memory of the dead man's face, lying on the gurney in the morgue. There was something about his face that struck a chord with me.

"What did you just say?" I asked.

She repeated herself.

"You're talking about Jesus Spares."

"Yes."

"Do you have any of the footage on your computer from the Split Down the Middle Event that took place here at the alley after Jesus Spares? Not the food fight videos that went viral. Just the regular recordings. Especially when people were entering the building and checking in for bowling."

"Yeah. I think I still have it. The state police made me keep it because of the governor being here."

Her eyes registered sadness as well as disappointment. For the record, Pastor Petula and Reverend Al had never been fully on board with the bowling for unity Split Down The Middle thing. Not that they were against the concept. Petula said she loved the idea of bringing people together. But she'd been uncomfortable, I could tell, around all of the politicians.

"Can you pull the video up for me to watch?" I asked.

"Okay," she said. "What are you looking for?"

"A face."

A minute later, we were watching the security camera footage from that afternoon.

I asked Petula to fast-forward it a little. The black-and-white video ran for about three or four minutes when I spotted him.

"There," I said.

She hit pause. Something about that image I was seeing struck a chord with me. Was it the hair? The body? The overall shape of his face?

"What you said about Jesus Spares triggered a memory," I explained. "The dead guy they called me in to ID the other day. I was bothered by that fact that, in addition to looking like Bo and me, something about him looked eerily familiar. I think it's his size, the shape of his face, and the fact that his arms and legs seem out of proportion to his torso. Then I remembered where I'd seen someone like that before. It was during the Split Down the Middle Conference. Except he must have disguised himself. His hair was much darker, and he had a dark mustache."

"You think it's the same as your dead lookalike guy? That he was at the conference?"

"I think so. I need to see if I can get ahold of an old mug shot of him."

"Well, that's no problem. An old photo of him is on the front page of the paper in a story about the murder. It's online too, think."

"Show me," I said.

She reached below the counter and pulled out the Partridgeberry newspaper. She held it up to her computer screen, and we studied it together. Although it was hard to see his whole body, what I could see confirmed my suspicion.

"I think it's the same man who's in the morgue," I said.

"Really? What does it mean?"

"I don't know, but it makes some sense. Whatever this guy was up to, he didn't just plan it and make it happen overnight. He must have shown up at the conference. Maybe to check out the overall situation."

"Maybe we should look at the registration and guest list."

"Don't worry about," I said. "I doubt he would have used his real name. Do you have any more security camera footage from that afternoon, the cameras that show the whole alley?"

"Yeah, I think so." She typed in some commands, and soon enough we were watching footage of the entire alley with the crowd of people milling about and bowling.

"Let's see if we can spot him again and see what he might have been doing."

We watched for several more minutes. We saw the disguised Etienne Bouchard on the video four more times. He wasn't bowling. Mostly he seemed to be just milling about talking with people in the crowd. But on three different occasions, he could clearly be seen hanging around the area where some of the TreadBo employees were working, and he was talking with some of them.

"Remember what you said to me the other day about the murder and Bo being arrested and all?" I asked.

"No." She shrugged. "Not exactly."

"Maybe you were just trying to be encouraging. But you said the answer could be right under my nose."

"I said that?"

"Yeah."

"Well"—she folded her arms—"it's true. Whenever I've been faced with a difficult situation and prayed about it, I've often found that to be case."

I smiled. "Thank you." Then I gave her a quick hug, kissed her on the forehead, and turned to go.

"For what?" she asked.

"You'll see," I said.

# 38

I was seated in the wooden chair across from my brother in the jail visiting room again. The deputy out front was watching Herk as she'd done before.

"How's it going?" I asked Bo through the phone.

The phone receiver to his ear, he stared at me through the thick glass. "I don't know, man." He looked thinner, like he hadn't eaten much of anything in days.

"Are you eating?" Bo was notoriously finicky about his diet.

"Not much. The food here's garbage."

"Even so. You should try to keep your strength up," I said, feeling like a mother hen.

"I try to choke down a little of it. Did you find the safe? Were my designs, drawings, and specification outlines okay?"

"I found the safe," I said, pausing a moment.

"And...?" Hunger must have made him even more impatient than usual.

"The safe was empty, Bo. There was nothing in it."

His gaze dropped away from mine. He seemed to shrink within himself, like a man who realized he was seeing a mirage.

"So you were right," I said. "Bouchard or somebody must have been after your new designs."

"Yeah. The question is, where are they now?"

I had no answer for that. "I should tell the sheriff about the new designs."

"Maybe," he said. "But if some company in China already has them, what difference will it make?"

"It will make a difference if it helps get you out of here."

"You remember those old reruns of *The Twilight Zone* we used to watch when we were kids?"

"Of course," I said.

"That's how I feel, Billy. Like I'm in an episode of an altered-reality show."

I said nothing.

"Have you heard anymore from Max Fontainebleau?" he asked.

"No. But my guess is he's still steamed about losing his money. I've been wondering if some of his old rumored mob friends might show to try break some bones or something, but there's been nothing."

"Can't believe he was so stupid to give away money like that. He should have known I would never come to him as an investor."

"Me either. Maybe his greed got the best of him. Bouchard could have promised him some great rate of return. He must have been pretty convincing if Fontainebleau really thought he was you. But listen. I found out something else that might be important."

"Yeah, what's that?" he said.

"Bouchard was at the Split Down the Middle Conference. That's probably when he started planning this thing, whatever it was. Not only that, Petula and I watched some footage of him that was recorded at the time by one of our security cameras at Split City. He seemed to be spending a lot of time chatting up some of your TreadBo employees."

"No kidding. You think someone from the factory is involved with this too?"

"Maybe."

"I have had to fire a couple of people over the years. Could be a disgruntled former employee I suppose."

"Do you remember their names?" I asked.

He nodded and gave them to me.

I wrote them down. "I'll also talk to the sheriff about Bouchard being at Split City for the conference. Not sure if it'll prove anything, but it might start help him looking in a better direction."

"Okay," he said. "You are always pushing, Billy, I'll give you that. All of those tournaments where you'd be so far behind after a couple of open frames…anybody else would've packed it in and just played out the string. But you, you wouldn't give up. Then, more often than not, you'd get on a tear. You'd get a five bagger and just keep rolling...strike after strike after strike after strike."

He continued, "We all knew it, the rest of us bowling against you. Whenever you'd get in the zone, you were going to punch out with all strikes. You could almost count on the exact score. It put the heat on everybody else, I'll tell you that. And a lot of times you'd win because of it. And even if you didn't, whoever was against you would be sweating bricks."

"Maybe that's what I need to do then. Put on some heat."

"Oh yeah? How are you going to do that?"

"I don't know," I admitted. "I'll try to think of something."

After Bo was taken back to his cell, I went to retrieve Herk from the deputy who'd been dog sitting him. I thanked her and turned to go. As I did, I couldn't help but notice a few stacks of folders and papers on an adjacent desk.

The title on one of the folders told me they were documents related to the Bouchard murder investigation—Bo's case. One piece of paper in particular had dislodged from its folder and was lying mostly visible on the desk. I realized it was the fake suicide note I'd heard about. I had a good look at the paper but didn't think much about it at the time.

# 39

Outside, the sun shone through the trees as I was heading toward the dunge with Herk panting happily along beside me. From the moment the sheriff showed me the TreadBo access card in the morgue, it had become more and more apparent that something wasn't right at TreadBo. Now I felt certain. If Bo was in the dark about Bouchard and what he'd been up to, there had to be someone else at TreadBo involved.

All I could think to do was head back over to the factory and start talking to people. I could get list of the names and contact info for all of the employees from Carianne. I was planning to blast some music—maybe Swedish House Mafia's "Don't You Worry Child"— through the 4Runner's anemic speakers on the way over to the factory to get myself psyched for whatever might happen.

I looked up to see Sheriff Lawton pulling into the lot behind the wheel of his dark-blue police cruiser.

"This ought to be interesting," I said to Herk.

He licked my hand and offered me a whimper.

"Don't worry, bud. They can't arrest two twin brothers at once."

I was making that last part up, of course.

The sheriff pulled into a space in front of the building.

I approached his car. He had sunglasses on but had pushed them up on top of his bald head as he powered down his window.

"I see you've still got your partner," he said.

"Therapy dog," I said.

"Huh. Join the club." He didn't elaborate, and I wasn't about to probe.

"Thanks for letting me bring him in the building when I'm visiting Bo."

He shrugged. "Look, I don't want you to get the wrong idea about me having to go and arrest your brother and all. None of this is personal. Murder's not something we see every day around here. And it's nothing any of us want to be messing around with."

I couldn't tell if that was veiled threat or a simple admission of the circumstances that had brought us to where we were. So I said nothing.

"He isn't guilty," I said.

He let out an exaggeration sigh, the kind of sound a parent makes when trying to deal with a rebellious teenager. "And you know this because….?" I couldn't help but notice he didn't reject the idea straightaway. I hoped he was beginning to have his doubts as well.

"I think whoever killed Bouchard was in cahoots with Bouchard. I think they were after a much bigger payday than just defrauding Fontainebleau. I think the money they stole from Fontainebleau was just a bonus."

"Oh, yeah? Interesting theory." He seemed to be considering it. "But the half a million dollars your brother and this lookalike may have stolen from Fontainebleau is a pretty big bonus, if you ask me. And what about this call to China? You have to admit, your brother has been involved with some crazy schemes in the past. Take what just happened at his so-called Split Down the Middle conference."

He folded his arms across his chest and looked at me. He was right, of course. But even as he tried to make his case, I could tell the sheriff was having big doubts. If what Bo said was accurate, his new designs and manufacturing specifications were worth a lot more than the Fontainebleau lost.

"What if Bo was working on some top-secret project that was going to rejuvenate TreadBo's fortunes? And what if Bouchard was actually trying to steal that? Which is why he was calling China before he was killed."

The sheriff stared at me. "Secret project, huh? Sounds like a reach. How do you know about this secret?"

"Bo told me about it. Yesterday."

"Right. In my experience, jail inmates say a lot of things. You have any evidence to support his claim?"

"Not yet. But what about Bo's phone?"

He let out a long sigh. "You might be right," he admitted. "I just got some off the phone with a technical supervisor at your brother's cell phone carrier. Turns out they think someone may have cloned your brother's phone. So to whoever he was calling, it was made to look like the calls were coming from Bo."

"Well, there you go then. That proves Bo's innocence, doesn't it?"

"Not so fast, Billy," he said. "This doesn't necessarily prove anything. Bo could have still been working with Bouchard. Let me ask you this: If your brother's big project was such a secret, how did Bouchard know about it?"

I looked at him for a long moment. "I can't say for sure," I said. "How about this for an idea: Maybe Bouchard somehow discovered he was a pretty close lookalike for Bo and me, and the more he looked into who Bo was, he saw an opportunity to pull off a big heist. You told me yourself he was involved with computer hacking. Maybe he infiltrated TreadBo's computers and accessed the camera on Bo's laptop. Maybe cloning the phone was part of a larger plan."

"That's a lot of maybes."

"I know. But TreadBo's computer guy, Mark Zune, also told me they've been having trouble with their servers. You could look into that."

"Don't worry," Lawton said. "We will."

"And since we know Bouchard was at the Split Down the Middle Conference, what if he'd been spying on Bo for some time?"

"What a minute," he said. "How do you know Bouchard was at the Split Down the Middle Conference?"

"Because I was just looking at him on some of our security camera footage from the event. I thought, when you asked me to identify him, something was familiar about his body and overall appearance besides being a lookalike with Bo and me. He'd colored his hair much darker at the conference and had a mustache, which must have been a fake."

"I want to see that footage," he said.

"Of course."

"So now you're speculating Bouchard had help."

"That's right."

"And you think this alleged partner was the one who killed him."

"Nothing else really makes sense, does it?" I still had no hard proof that Bo hadn't been the killer, but it felt like I was edging closer and closer to the truth.

"Why would Bouchard's partner kill him?" he asked. "Why not just split this big payoff you're talking about, along with the money from Fontainebleau, between the two of them, and run?"

"I don't know," I admitted. "Could've been lots of different reasons. Maybe the killer got greedy. Maybe something went wrong."

"Mmm…" The sheriff still seemed skeptical. Although I could see he was seriously considering the possibility.

"All right," he said. "I'm willing to give you the benefit of the doubt for now. I'm still leaning toward your brother's guilt. And since I've tried warning you off and you don't appear to be stopping, let me also give you some free advice."

"It's a free country," I said.

"This is serious business."

"You don't have to tell me it is."

"No, I mean it. Scriblow and I are still investigating," he said. "That doesn't stop just because someone's been arrested, charged, and arraigned. And I'm willing to admit if I've been wrong or missed something along the way. But you also need to think long and hard about why you're doing what you're doing."

"Why is that?" I asked.

"Because if what you just proposed is true, or any part of it, then we're looking at a killer who's still on the loose."

# 40

With that cheery warning from the sheriff ringing in my ears, I loaded Herk in the dunge and headed for the TreadBo factory. Maybe I'd convinced him I was on the right track. Maybe not. At least he seemed to be warming to the idea.

I also began to think.

If Bouchard had been stalking Bo online for a while, hijacked some of his cameras, and figured out how potentially valuable his new design plans were, it stood to reason he might have tried to recruit an insider, someone who worked at TreadBo, to help carry out his plot to steal the plans.

But what motive did the insider have? Money? Anger at Bo? Revenge?

Perhaps a disgruntled former employee had teamed up with Bouchard as Bo had suggested. Or it could have been a current worker. Either way, if there was a traitor and a killer among the TreadBo employees or former employees, he or she might not be that easy to find without tipping them off.

TreadBo, as far as I knew, currently employed nearly seventy people. It could take days for me to track down and interview each one of them. Given what I knew, maybe it would be best to stakeout the factory while I thought about my next move.

An hour later, Herk and I had set up camp beside a dirt road on a hillside at the base of Blackfish Mountain. From our hidden perch, we had a panoramic view of the TreadBo factory a couple of hundred yards below.

"Settle in, pal," I said. "This might take a while."

Luckily, I'd brought along a fresh box of crispy biscuit treats and a couple of oversized rawhide chewy bones that looked like they came from some storybook movie set featuring dinosaurs. After the first few minutes, I let Herk have at the first one. That, I figured, ought to be good for a couple of hours.

For the next couple of hours, we watched and waited. The sky turned gunmetal gray. Before too long, Mark Zune exited the main entrance below, roaring off in his blue all-wheel-drive SUV. Carianne left soon after Zune, looking stoic as she climbed into her practical gray Nissan. The factory was otherwise completely dark and silent.

Finally, around 5:00 p.m., an older sedan pulled in front of the building. I scanned the windshield with my binoculars and noticed a young woman I didn't recognize behind the wheel. Ralph Warrens stepped out of the front door of the factory, locking it behind him and making sure it was secure, before looking over the building.

He stepped down from the curb, opened the door of the sedan, and climbed into the front passenger seat. He said something to the young woman, and they drove off together.

I fished my cell phone from my pocket and dialed Carianne's mobile number. She answered after a couple of rings.

"Hi, Billy. Is everything okay?"

"Yeah. Can I ask you something?"

"Sure. Anything."

"Does Ralph have a younger girlfriend or something?"

"Who, Ralph?" She laughed. "No. Of course not. Why?"

"I don't know. I just happened to notice he was picked up by someone from work just now, and there was a much-younger woman behind the wheel."

"Oh. That must be his daughter. She and Ralph's granddaughter have been living with him for the past couple of months. Ralph must have let her use his car."

"Oh. All right. I was just curious. That's all."

"You sure you're okay?"

"Yeah. I'm fine. Thanks for the info."

"No problem. Anytime. You take care."

He nodded and stood to go. "Aren't you leaving, too?"

#

Herk and I watched and waited another half an hour. Still, nothing happened. Yet I couldn't shake the feeling I was closing in on a killer. I just didn't know how or why.

"C'mon, buddy," I said to Herk finally. "It's getting too dark to see. Time to go."

As I stood to leave, my cell phone rang in my pocket. I pulled it out and looked at the display. Justine again. Great. Hearing the voice of my ex-girlfriend again was the last thing I needed right now.

I was almost going to let it go to voicemail but changed my mind.

"Billy? Is that you?" she asked.

"Yeah."

"I'm coming home tomorrow night," she said. "And I want to come pick up Herk."

"Uh, not right now, Justine. I think I'm going to keep him a while longer."

"What!"

She obviously didn't take kindly to being crossed.

"He's a comforting presence, and I need him right now more than you," I said.

"But—" She started to let loose with a string of insults, but I cut her off as I noticed the beams from a pair of headlights as a vehicle swung into the TreadBo parking lot below.

"Sorry, Justine, but I can't talk right now. I'll touch base with you when you get back," I said before ending the call.

Was this what I'd been waiting for?

I reached for the binoculars and zoomed in on the vehicle. It was Carianne's car. Had she forgotten something?

I watched as she pulled in front of the building and parked. Then she climbed out and went to the front door. She unlocked it and reentered the building. A light came on in the stairwell and a couple of moments later upstairs in the offices.

What was she up to?

There was only one way to find out.

# 41

Herk and I barreled down the narrow road toward the factory. Chances were the reason she'd returned had nothing to do with the killing or Bo being in jail. On the other hand, Carianne was exactly the type of insider who had access to enough information about Bo and TreadBo to have been involved with whatever Bouchard was doing. She also might know more than she'd been letting on. Maybe I should be asking her some more pointed questions.

The front door was unlocked. The lobby stood quiet and empty as Herk and I entered the building. Upstairs, we found Carianne seated as per usual at her desk, however.

"This place feels almost like the morgue," I said, doing my best to sound casual.

She looked up with a start. "Oh, hi, Billy. Hi, Herk." She reached out to pet the big retriever, who responded with an affectionate lean into her hand. "Yeah, it's pretty dead around here with the temporary factory shutdown. At least, I hope it's just temporary."

"But you're still here."

"Yeah," she said with a sigh. "I went home for a while but came back. I don't know if any of us are going to be getting paid or not, but I have few things to tidy up, and," she added, looking sheepish, "to be honest, this computer's better than the one I have at home to update my resume."

I glanced at her computer screen and saw her resume, which she wasn't trying to hide.

"No arguments from me there," I said. "Can't say as I blame you."

"What are you doing here?" she asked.

"Actually, I came by looking for something," I said, not wanting her to suspect anything.

"Oh. What's that?"

I needed to think fast.

Watching the parking lot that afternoon had made me think about cars and trucks. I was reminded about what the sheriff told me about the broken glass and evidence of an accident between two vehicles that had been found near Bouchard's dead body.

"Do you keep any kind of a record of the vehicles your employees drive?" I asked. "You know, for parking and security purposes."

"Uh, yeah, sure," she said. "Parking's usually not an issue, but every now then there's been a problem with kids using the lot on weekends for drinking or making out. It's not very high-tech. I think Ralph keeps the list on a clipboard in his desk down in the lobby."

"Is the desk open?"

"No, I think he keeps it locked."

"Do you by any chance have an extra key to Ralph's desk so I can go get the list?"

"I think so," she said. "Seems like people are always losing their key cards around here. So, I've had extra cards and an extra set of keys made." She opened one of her lower drawers and rummaged through a stack of papers until she found a key ring she kept in the back of the drawer. She went through the keys until she found the right one, removed it from the key ring, and handed it to me.

I went back downstairs. Inside I found a clipboard with a neatly typed sheet of paper that listed the name, address, and phone number for all TreadBo employees, as well as an accompanying list of vehicle makes and license plate numbers. I took the list, intending to make a copy upstairs before replacing the original.

Heading back up the stairs with Herk, I absently scanned the alphabetical parking list for Ralph's name. His was listed with the others on the second page. It showed his home address, license plate number, and the make of his car. It wasn't a sedan, as I'd assumed from seeing him picked up by his daughter the day before. The vehicle listed for Ralph was a late-model pickup truck.

*Huh*, I thought. *Interesting.*

Back upstairs, I showed the list to Carianne.

"What's wrong?" she asked.

"Remember I called you a little while ago because I saw Ralph's daughter driving with him yesterday?"

"Yes."

"They were in an old sedan. But that's not the type of car listed under his name here on the parking roster."

"Oh. I don't think that's Ralph's car. It's probably belongs to his daughter. Ralph drives a pickup truck."

"Then why weren't they driving Ralph's pickup?"

"I have no idea...no, wait. Come to think about it, he told me day before yesterday his truck was in the shop because he had a run-in with a deer. You know how it is. Happens all the time around here. Especially during mating season when the big bucks are all crazed and chasing after the does."

"You're telling me Ralph said he hit a deer with his truck the other day."

"Yeah," she said. "What's wrong?"

I must have had a strange look on my face because it was beginning to dawn on me that something might not be right about Ralph.

Glancing around her office, I noticed a large clear plastic container tucked in a corner behind some files. Taped to the outside of the container was a photo of a pretty little girl and a handwritten note. Inside the container there was some cash and a couple of checks.

"Are you collecting money for something?" I asked.

"Oh, yeah. That. It's for Ralph's granddaughter," she said. "Poor thing. She's only eight years old and has some kind of rare disease that can be fatal. Apparently, there aren't even approved medications or treatments for whatever she has in the US, and they have to try to take her to Europe for medical care, which her health insurance won't cover." She paused. "Ralph's pretty stoic. He doesn't like to talk about it. But one of the factory guys found out, so we've been collecting a little money to try to help."

"I'm sorry to hear about that," I said, my mind on something else.

I was reflexively starting to fish a twenty out of my wallet to stick in the container when the solution as to who killed Etienne Bouchard came together for me.

Petula had said something to me a couple of days before. The explanation for Bo's innocence was probably something simple—it might be right in front of me.

I knew Bouchard had been at the Split Down the Middle Conference the month before. He'd been there to stake out the situation regarding the crime he was planning, no doubt. But he also might have been there to strike up a relationship with someone from

TreadBo to see if he could recruit an ally to make his task easier.

That ally needed a motive.

And Ralph Warrens needed money for to pay for his granddaughter's treatment—apparently lots of money.

But that wasn't all. The sheriff had told me Bouchard's car was missing. He said they'd found evidence of a collision. Apparently, Ralph's truck was now said to be in shop.

What if he'd been the one that had struck Bouchard's car because something went wrong on their deal?

What clinched it for me, however, was something else I remembered.

When I'd seen Ralph writing the note to his granddaughter the other day, I'd noticed he was carefully folding a piece of paper. He'd said something about making paper airplanes for his granddaughter, and I'd seen the creases on the paper he was folding.

It dawned on me that I'd just seen those same kinds of creases and folds again.

It'd been on the fake suicide note I'd caught a glance of at the sheriff's office. Even the paper was the same.

When it came to Bouchard, the dead lookalike in the morgue, we'd all been thinking about a murder. But what if there had been no murderer? What if there was only a grandfather? A grandfather driven to desperation. A grandfather who may have killed in self-defense or by accident.

Still, I had no solid proof.

"Are you okay, Billy?" Carianne asked.

She must have noticed the sudden change in my demeanor.

"Never mind," I said. "I gotta go."

# 42

But wouldn't you know? On the verge of my first great sleuthing triumph, my plan began to go haywire.

All seemed well enough at first.

I dialed Sheriff Lawton on the way back to my car. He picked up after a couple of rings.

"I'm beginning to regret I gave you this number," he said.

"I've got good news," I told him. "I think I know who killed Bouchard. And it isn't Bo."

An audible sigh sounded through the phone.

"I'm listening," he said, finally.

"Meet me at this location in fifteen minutes, and I'll explain everything." I read off Ralph Warren's address listed on the parking roster.

"And what, pray tell, am I going to find at this magical spot?" he asked.

"I'm hoping a desperate person and not a real killer."

Silence.

Another sigh.

"I'm way up county at the moment," he said. "The address you gave me is in Partridgeberry. It may take me a while to get there." I heard him punching keys on his laptop.

"Just come as fast as you can."

"Wait a sec." He was apparently getting more information from his computer. "This is Ralph Warren's place, Billy. What gives?"

"You'll see," I said.

"Okay," he said. "But you better not be wasting my time."

Herk and I jumped into the dunge. I threw the SUV into gear and made a beeline for the parking lot exit.

That was when the fun started.

Before I could reach the street, a dark Mercedes sedan appeared out of nowhere to block my path.

Both front car doors flew open, and two heavy-set young men with dark curly hair, who looked like they'd just come straight from lifting weights at the gym, jumped out. They wore black city jeans and black leather jackets. They were brandishing dark Glock pistols like they'd just finished shooting an episode of *Lethal Weapon.*

What now? I couldn't help but roll my eyes.

I braked to a halt in front of them. One of them motioned for me to step out of my truck. I wasn't about to leave the relative safety and cover of the vehicle, however. I powered down my driver's window instead.

"Mr. Gills," one of them said. "Like to have a word with you."

"What do you want?"

"We're associates of Mr. Max Fontainebleau."

"Associates?" I raised a skeptical eyebrow.

One of them, who must have fancied himself the lead henchman, managed to gargle out a few words. "Uh. Er…Well, not exactly. We're his nephews. By marriage."

"Does Mr. Fontainebleau know you're here?"

"Not exactly. Not yet anyway. But we'd like to discuss how Mr. Fontainebleau, besides being your landlord, is going to get his money back from you and your brother, Mr. Gill."

"I hope he told you I had nothing to do with that."

"Yeah, well, see, Mr. Gills, that's where things get kind of confusing. Something about you being an identical twin and all, and your brother being in jail."

They must have had very polite mobsters wherever Max Fontainebleau was from.

I looked at Herk panting unconcerned in the seat next to me. "Some guard dog you are."

Herk didn't seem to take offense. He kept panting softly. Maybe he didn't see these two wannabe gangsters as much of threat.

I turned back to them. "Look, I can show you exactly where Max can get his money."

"You know where it is, then?"

"Absolutely," I lied. "I'll take you there right now."

He squinted at me as if he were trying to read my poker face. Then he fished a phone from his pocked and dialed while the other goon held his gun on me. He turned his head away and spoke quietly into the phone. Then he hung up and turned back to me.

"You ride with us," he said. "Take us there."

"No deal," I said.

Carianne was still in the building, working at her computer. I looked around the lot to see if any potential help or other witnesses might be around, but there was no one else.

"I'll tell you what," I said. "How about we do this? I'll drive my truck with my dog here, and you can follow in your nice big car there. You see me do anything suspicious or try to speed off, you can shoot out my tires…or whatever it is you people do."

His squint got worse. "Seems to me you're in no position to be bargaining, Mr. Gills."

"All right then. I've got my foot right next to the accelerator. I see you left me a slight opening to slip past your fancy car, or I may cause a little damage to it—who knows? You really want to start shooting right here in town? Probably going to be more than one witness. That wouldn't make County Supervisor

Fontainebleau so happy. Or would you rather just do as I ask and follow me quietly to go get Max's money?"

He worked his jaw back and forth like he was choking on a chicken bone or a piece of steak. He didn't seem too pleased with my proposition. On the other hand, I was also hoping he wasn't as stupid as he looked.

"All right, Gills," he said. "But when we get to where we are going, I want you out of that truck. Your dog, too."

Uh-oh. I was pretty sure the man had just threatened my dog. I had half a mind to run him down right then and there.

But I didn't think that would necessarily contribute to me solving Etienne Bouchard's murder and becoming a hero.

"Whatever you say, gentlemen," I said.

# 43

Ralph Warrens' house hardly looked like the home of a coldblooded killer.

The small bungalow stood behind a white picket fence on a tree-lined side street not far from the TreadBo factory. Green shoots sprouted from a pair of window flower boxes. A garden hose was attached to the side of the house, and there was an oversized garage with a storage shed in back. The small sedan I'd seen Ralph picked up in the day before sat in the driveway.

I'd kept my Mercedes mafia friends in my rearview mirror the whole way.

Arriving in front of the house, I saw Sheriff Lawton had yet to arrive.

I pulled to the curb and sent the sheriff a quick text, careful to keep my hands out of sight of my armed escort: *URGENT. COULD USE SOME IMMEDIATE HELP.*

Swift came his reply: *DON'T DO ANYTHING STUPID. BE THERE BEFORE TOO LONG.*

*Before too long.*

What was that supposed to mean? Ten minutes? Twenty?

I wasn't sure how long I could stall the goons behind me.

I took a moment to gather my thoughts. I was here to catch a killer, and Ralph didn't know I knew what I did about his truck or the folds in the papers on his desk. Maybe I could use these two fools in the car behind me to my advantage. The two goombahs might throw Ralph off guard. Or they might at least sow enough confusion to keep him from running until the sheriff arrived.

"Herk. You stay here and stay safe, pal. Just lie on the seat and wait like a good dog."

Herk apparently decided he didn't want to lie down. He licked my ear and the side of my face.

"All right," I said. "Have it your way. Just try to stay quiet."

Before reaching for the car door, I activated the voice recording app on my cell phone. I tucked it the front pocket of my jeans, hoping I wasn't about to be recording my own demise.

I was barely out of the truck and closing the door behind me before the Fontainebleau nephews stood by my side. Herk erupted, barking rather loudly at the sight of me between the two idiots. So much for remaining quiet.

"This better be good, Mr. Gills," the older one snarled.

"Oh, it'll be good. I promise."

"Looks like your animal there is a real killer," the younger goon guffawed. Apparently, he didn't think much of golden retrievers. Maybe he'd forgotten to feed his pet python. At least they weren't dumb enough to still be brandishing their Glocks.

"This doesn't look the kind of a place we're going to get Uncle Max his money back," the older one said in a fit of brilliant observance.

"Appearances can be deceiving," I said.

He said nothing. Herk continued barking. They accompanied me through the gate and up to the front porch.

"So we just going to break the door down and storm into this place?" the younger one asked. Apparently, he was itching for some action. Probably from watching too many Spider Man movies.

"No," I said. "We're going to ring the doorbell like real people do."

"Cool it, Ritchie," the older one said. "Let's see how this thing plays out."

A storm door opened to a heavier front door. I left them alone and pressed the doorbell button attached to the doorframe.

We waited. Nothing happened.

"No one home," the older one said. "This better not be some kind of a scam."

At that point the front door opened a crack and a mousy young woman's face appeared in the opening behind a chain lock. "Can I help you gentleman?" Her voice was muffled a bit by the storm door.

"Yes," I said. "I'm looking for Ralph Warrens."

"He's…he's not home," she blurted out—so quickly it was obvious she was lying.

"I see. Do you know where he is or when he's coming back?"

"No, I—"

"It's okay, Mindy." I heard Ralph's voice behind her. "I got it."

A large hand I recognized as Ralph's appeared at the edge of the door. His face appeared in the opening. I heard the voice of a child calling out from somewhere in the house. His daughter disappeared.

Ralph eyed the two goombahs with suspicion. "What's this all about, Billy?"

"Well, I wanted to ask you a few more questions about the man who was killed here recently and about my brother being in jail." My heart pounded in my chest. Still no sign of the sheriff.

He looked at me, squinting. "Who are these two clowns?"

"They tell me they're Max Fontainebleau's nephews."

"Fontainebleau. Nephews, huh? What do they want?"

I ignored the questions.

"Ralph," I began, "I heard your pickup is in the shop for repair. Carianne said you ran into a deer?"

"Yeah? So? What's that go to do with why you're here?"

"I'm going to go out on a limb here, Ralph. I don't think you hit any deer with your truck. I think you crashed into someone else's car. I think that was someone whose dead face looks an awful lot like Bo and me."

He glared at me but said nothing.

So, it looked like I was right. At least about some of it. Maybe event most of it.

Which, while a relief, came with a big concern. Namely, the two nephews standing behind me who obviously had no idea what was going on. This wasn't exactly how I'd pictured my big crime-solving moment going down.

I kept going.

"The sheriff told me there was broken glass and evidence of an accident where Bouchard's body was found," I said. "I found out your truck had been in an accident. Then I heard about your granddaughter's condition. The need for money for her travel and treatment. And I discovered Bouchard had been at the

Split Down the Middle Conference last month. Was that when he first approached you, or was it before?"

He didn't dispute anything I'd said. I hoped I could keep him talking until help arrived, but his demeanor darkened. I took a step back.

Then, before any of us on the porch realized what was happening, Ralph turned and looked away. The sharp chu-chack of a pump action shotgun being chambered split the air.

"What the—" one of the thugs managed to spit out.

But it was too late for him or anyone else to react. The nose of a twelve gauge was already pointing out at us through the partly open door.

# 44

I raised my hands in the air.

I couldn't see behind me, but apparently the idiot nephews were too scared to even move, let alone reach for their guns.

"Get your hands up, numbnuts," the older nephew was saying to the younger one.

"You people need to get away from my house," Ralph said.

"Hold on, old man." The second nephew still didn't want to back down.

"Take it easy, Ralph," I said. "You don't want to make things worse than they already are."

"It's not what you think it is, Billy."

"It's not?"

"No. You're right. I killed that Bouchard, if that's what his real name was. But I had to. He came at me after I tried to stop him."

"Stop him from what?"

Once more, I thought as long as I could keep him talking until the sheriff got there, we might just have a chance.

"He promised me he would cover all of the experimental treatment and travel expenses for my granddaughter," Ralph said. "He said he was getting a bunch of money through TreadBo but that it was only TreadBo's insurance company that would lose out. I wasn't sure what he was up to, but all I had to do was leave the front door open and an all-access key card on my desk. He approached me, like you said, at the conference. After that I only communicated with him online. Until the other night, that is."

I hoped the phone in my pocket was still recording and getting all of this.

"Why'd you try to stop him then?" I asked.

"I didn't fully trust him. Plus, I was having second thoughts. So I decided to keep watch when he showed up at the factory. I parked my truck behind the building and hid inside. When I saw how he looked—like you and your brother—I was kind of shocked. I found him in Bo's office. There was a safe hidden in the floor there I didn't know about. He'd taken some things from it, money and some documents, and was closing it up and putting the floorboards back. I asked him what he was doing, and he told me not to worry, it wasn't my concern. But I smelled a rat, and I told him to stop. He ran out of the building with the papers and the money. I gave chase and he went for his car. He was too fast for me, but my truck was already idling at the curb."

"Was that how he ended up next to the warehouses down the street?"

"Yes. I caught up with him there. Rammed his car and jumped out. We fought, and he pulled a gun. I managed to get it away from him, but it went off and shot him in the head."

"So you panicked and tried to make it look like a suicide."

"Yeah. Believe me, Billy, I never in a million years thought somebody would try to blame Bo for what happened."

"What happened to Bouchard's car?" I asked.

"I drove it into the river."

"What about the papers and the money?"

"The papers look like some kind of new shoe designs Bo's been working on. I figured that's what the guy had really been up to. They're right inside here. On my kitchen table with the money."

"Wow. That's quite a story there, Sparky," the older nephew said, apparently recovering some of his arrogant stupidity. "What is this, Gills? Some kind of a trick? You said we were going to get our uncle's money back for us."

I looked the wannabe thug in the eyes. "What is it with you two? Were you born with some kind of a death wish? The man here's pointing a shotgun at us, and he clearly knows how to use it."

Ralph made a loud noise clearing his throat. "Look, fellas. I don't know what's going on with you and these people, Billy, and it's been fun chatting with you. But it's time for me to go. And I'm taking my daughter and granddaughter with me."

"Where are you going to go, Ralph?"

"Over the border. Away from all of this. We're packed and ready to go. I've already written a confession and mailed it to the sheriff's office."

Speaking of the sheriff, where in the world was he? What was taking him so long?

At that moment, a truck engine roared from the back of the house. Ralph slammed the door shut and bolted it behind him.

"Holy crap!" the younger nephew shouted. "You're just going to let him go?"

"Not if I can help it," I said.

I bolted toward the porch railing. I leaped over it in the direction of the driveway, surprising myself, doing my best to land and roll in the soft grass without breaking an ankle.

Rising to my feet, I turned to see Ralph running out the back door with his shotgun and jumping into the passenger seat of a truck, which had to be his, judging by the damage to the front end. The truck was emerging from a garage as the door opened.

Ralph's daughter who'd been at the door earlier was driving the truck. I could also see a child that must have been Ralph's granddaughter seated in back.

The two nephews, confused and slower, were coming around the front steps next to me with guns in hand.

"Put those guns away!" I yelled at them.

What was I planning to do? Throw myself in front of the truck, action hero-style?

I had no idea.

To my surprise, however, the Fontainebleau nephews immediately complied. They tucked their guns back in their jackets and stopped in their tracks.

Glancing toward the street, I saw why. The *whoop-whoop* of a siren sounded as a state police cruiser with its lights whirling raced into view. The car screeched to a halt, and out jumped former wrestling legend Sergeant Rachel Maracle and another trooper.

Maracle drew her pearl-handled .45 semiautomatic. "Hands up! Everyone on the ground! I want everyone's hands where I can see them!" Her big gun swept back and forth, pointed at the three of us.

I started to lie down, and out of the corner of my eye I saw the two nephews doing the same as the other trooper moved in with his gun drawn and pointed at them as well. Then an engine roared as Ralph's truck lurched forward.

Maracle stepped directly in its path and directed her aim at the windshield. "You in the truck, show me your hands! Show your hands!"

The truck ground to a halt.

Ralph and his daughter raised their hands.

A second later, Sheriff Lawton's cruiser careened into the driveway as well. The doors flew open, and the sheriff and Mac Mallen came out with their handguns drawn.

I started to rise, but Mac stopped me.

"Stay down, Billy. Just stay down there," he told me. "This is for your own safety until we get this all sorted out. Hands behind your back."

So much for my reward for being a great detective.

I did as he instructed. A few seconds later, he pulled a plastic zip tie snuggly around my wrists, and, from the sounds of it, it appeared the other state trooper was doing the same with the Fontainebleau nephews.

It's not easy to tell what's going on around you when you're lying facedown on the ground with your hands zip tied behind your back and your cheek in the cold grass. The sheriff apparently got Ralph and his daughter out of the truck and on the ground as well. I could hear the granddaughter crying in the back seat.

I heard another vehicle pull to the curb. Turning my head, I saw Max Fontainebleau storming toward us.

"What's going's on here! What do you two idiots think you're doing? Not you, trooper, I'm talking about my fool nephews here."

"Well, Mr. Fontainebleau," Sergeant Maracle said, "your two young relatives here are under arrest."

"Under arrest?" Fontainebleau tried to turn his bluster on her. "What's the charge?"

"What are you all up in my business for?" She waved the pistol menacingly. "Back off."

Fontainebleau took a step back as if she'd just maxi-slapped him into next week.

"My apologies, Sergeant...whatever your name is. Looks like my two sweet nephews here were just trying to play the role of vigilantes."

"Yeah, that's right," the younger blurted out. "We're vigilantes. We're trying to help this guy here capture a killer."

"Oh, is that right?" I said, my voice dripping with sarcasm.

"Stay out of this, Max," Sheriff Lawton warned, "until we get this figured out."

I turned my head again and saw Maracle patting down the nephews and removing the two Glocks they'd tucked into their waistbands. She handcuffed them both. Then she yanked the first to one his feet with a single hand like he was little more than a bag of chew toys for the pet wolves I would one day find out she kept on her property.

Turning to Lawton, she said, "Thanks for the tip. These two half-wits have been causing problems all over the state. We've been after them for a while."

"My pleasure," he said.

"You two gentlemen"—she yanked the second handcuffed one to his feet as easily as she had the first—"are under arrest for grand theft auto."

"What?! You numbskulls have been out stealing cars?" Fontainebleau roared at them. "I told you if that happened again, I wasn't having nothing more to do with you."

"Shut up, Max," the sheriff said. Fontainebleau complied.

Deputy Mallen said nothing. He went about the rest of his work silently and efficiently. He patted me down and took my phone.

Herk was still barking his head off behind the windows in my 4Runner. Ralph's granddaughter was still wailing away in the back of Ralph's truck. After everyone was secured and all was quiet, I turned my head toward the driveway again and saw Sheriff Lawton coming my way.

"Now, Billy," he said, looming over me like the final judgment, "you want to explain to me what in the blue blazes is going on here with Ralph?"

# 45

"Billy…you ready to bowl?"

I heard Reverend Al's voice before I saw him. His deep bass and easy tone were impossible to miss.

I wiped a bead of sweat from my forehead. I was in the back of the kitchen at Split City making sandwiches, helping some of our part-time workers put together more trays of food to feed the hungry masses that had descended on the alley for the next Jesus Spares event.

Petula toiled joyfully away at the reception desk, assigning bowling lanes. She'd enlisted G's help checking out bowling shoes (mostly TreadBo, of course).

Al appeared from around the corner. As I said before, he was a big man, a former college athlete. His full black beard and curly black hair framed a ready smile.

"Sorry to interrupt, but everybody's waiting for you," he said.

Jesus Spares had filled Split City with a cacophonous assortment of people. They'd come from all walks of life, from all races and backgrounds, young and old—from Partridgeberry, Madaga, and beyond. They'd showed up seeking free food, free bowling, laughter, and fun—and for some, maybe even some measure of truth and forgiveness. This particular Sunday, there seemed to be plenty of forgiveness, smiles, and laughter to go around.

It had been more than two weeks since Ralph Warrens had been arrested for killing Etienne Bouchard. Bo had been released from the county jail. All charges against him had been dropped. He'd even gotten his secret new shoe designs and specifications back. (It turned out Ralph had confronted Bouchard in the middle of his attempt to transmit the files to his illicit overseas partners. The transmission of the stolen design documents had apparently never gone through.)

Max Fontainebleau was still trying to get his half a million dollars back. His lawyers were apparently "very optimistic." He said they'd assured him the obstacles blocking Fontainebleau from accessing the offshore account where Bouchard had deposited the purloined funds could be overcome and that our grotesquely intrepid county supervisor would get most of his money back. Minus his lawyers' hefty fee of course.

As for Ralph Warrens, the case was now in the hands of our county prosecutor. Deputy Mallen told me the evidence the sheriff's department had gathered so far seemed to indicate that Ralph had a strong case for self-defense when it came to the killing of Bouchard. But despite his motives, Ralph had also clearly committed a crime. He never should have agreed to help Bouchard. Rumor had it, there might be a plea bargain in the wind. As long as Ralph plead guilty to conspiracy to commit insurance fraud, the hope was, he'd be sentenced to probation or a short in-home incarceration. Given the extenuating circumstances, it seemed like appropriate punishment.

Out in the alley, Jesus Spares rolled on.

The music was upbeat: a mixture of gospel, rock, some old-time hymns, and even a little rap at times. Among the crowd, faithful worshipers shook hands and joined in conversation with a smattering of off-season tourists and a gaggle of elderly folks from the local assisted-living facility (some formally dressed and others in bathrobes pushing walkers).

The throng also included several people in their twenties and thirties, families with children and teens, a few questionable-looking strangers, and even a handful of inmates from the nearby state minimum-security prison camp who'd been allowed to attend with their guards. People ate and talked and ate some more. Many were also beginning to bowl.

Around Twin Strikes, word had quickly gotten out about everything that had happened at TreadBo with Ralph. Not everyone had their facts straight about him killing a man, but almost everyone understood that Missy Warren, Ralph's granddaughter, needed help.

So, the local community had banded together for a fundraising drive to help pay for Missy's experimental cancer treatment. As part of that effort, a banner hung from the ceiling of Split City that afternoon indicating the day's Jesus Spares event was part of the Help Missy Warren campaign. I was pretty sure Bo had already contributed a large personal check on top of the one he'd already put in the fundraising jar at the factory the month before.

The idea behind the Bo vs. Billy exhibition game was that people could place a friendly donation wager on which twin brother would win. Those contributors who picked the winner would have their contributions to the Help Missy Warren campaign matched by TreadBo.

Out of the corner of my eye, I caught sight of Bo warming up on one of the far lanes.

"You ready, big guy?" I called out to him.

He smiled and gave me a thumbs-up. "Just scraping some of the rust off of my game. Trying some new grips and approaches."

As far as I knew, Bo hadn't bowled in front of people in at least five years.

"I don't want to hear any excuses now," I teased him.

"Okay, I'll try to remember that when I win, and my team raises the most money."

Bo. Ever the over-striding inventor.

Not that I was infused with a great deal of confidence, considering the way I'd been bowling of late. I'd already decided to ignore my competitive instinct today. Whichever one of us won, it was all for a good cause.

After donning my shoes, I took my ball out of its bag and wiped it down. Stepping to the nearest empty lane, I rolled a couple of practice frames myself.

One strike. One almost spare. Not too bad.

Petula soon appeared and got things organized.

A crowd began to swell around the two lanes where Bo and I would be bowling. A few people were still making last-minute donation wagers, and, from what I could tell, the betting was pretty evenly divided. Which was fine by me.

Bo and I laughed and shook hands. Smartphones snapped photos.

"This should be fun," I said.

"You bet." He smiled at his corny pun.

And so, the game began.

We each opened with strikes. Mine had a nice controlled hook to it—right into the pocket. Bo's did too. Causing me to wonder for a moment if he had been secretly practicing somewhere on the side.

Then we settled into the rhythm of the next few frames. Bo reverted to his careful, analytical style of bowling—the opposite of his eccentric personality. He was consistent: precise on his strikes, and never missing a spare. I, on the other hand, found myself whipsawing back and forth between excellence and mediocrity. I missed a number of strikes by a wide margin. I even bowled an open frame.

#

By the midway point, I found myself twenty pins down. Some in the crowd were becoming restless. When I missed the spare, I heard an audible groan. I looked over at Bo. He was all concentration.

I decided then and there to let it all go. To forget about the result and just bowl. A feeling of peace washed over me. And I started to throw strikes. Strike after strike after strike.

Bo was the first one to recognize the shift. He grinned and gave me a nod.

I kept rolling strikes. Although his lead was shrinking, Bo kept the pressure up. He remained consistent, and it all came down to the final frame. After Bo finished, a quick calculation showed me I had no chance of winning and needed to finish with three straight strikes to even manage a tie. Everyone else seemed to have figured out the same thing, and all went silent throughout the alley.

All right then, I decided. This is my home turf. Split City. Time to let it roll.

One strike. Two. Then three.

When my last ball exploded the pins, the crowd erupted into applause and cheers.

The final score was 219 to 219.

"How did that happen?" I said to Bo.

He shook his head. He couldn't stop smiling, and neither could I.

When Bo announced in a loud voice the tie meant TreadBo was going to match everyone's donation to the Help Missy Warren Fund, the cheers grew louder and louder. Up and down the lanes. In the kitchen and the restaurant.

As the applause continued, Bo and I stood side by side, arms around each other's shoulder and took a bow. I looked out over Split City and couldn't help but think in that moment how everyone there had become, for those fleeting moments at least, part of one family. One giant hot mess of humanity that had come together for a worthwhile cause.

And something else happened when I was bowling that final frame. Something I've never, to this day, told anyone else.

I felt strangely out of my body. Even focused on those pins, I was able to look around the alley and see things then I shouldn't have, logically, been able to see. Not just the crowd, but each individual.

I saw Petula, smiling as she watched from the back corner with Herk standing next to her. I saw G—for once, looking contented. Across the way, I spotted Sheriff Lawton (who'd shown up along with Deputy Mallen), and Deputy Scriblow, nodding with satisfaction. And I caught sight of several people from TreadBo, too—Carianne, Zune, Addison Foley, and others. They were looking on and seemed to be smiling with a newfound curiosity at their boss.

I even spied Max Fontainebleau, arms crossed and chomping on a cigar; he seemed to be chuckling at some private joke with himself. On the other side of the crowd, I saw State Trooper Sergeant Bluewind Maracle, whose eyes shone with so much excitement she could have been transported back to her professional wrestling days. Next to Maracle stood Aubrey Brown, who seemed surrounded by a kind of love I wanted to know.

And last, but not least, I could see my parents, Wilson and Gertrude Gills. They were laughing together in the background as if recalling a fond memory. Standing someplace separate but altogether present—like their personal bowling balls behind the glass display in my office.

I may not be sure about a lot of things, but I know what I saw that afternoon at Jesus Spares.

Sometimes, I can't help but wonder if it might have been a picture of what's to come.

Printed in the USA
CPSIA information can be obtained
at www.ICGtesting.com
JSHW012020140824
68134JS00033B/2798